"What do
want a ma

Henry shifted the baby to his shoulder, patting him lightly on the back. It was amazing how quickly he was adapting to this whole fatherhood thing.

"So, what's the little guy's answer?" Henry hadn't heard Charli approach.

He caught her gaze and held it for a long moment. There was no doubt in her eyes.

Could he really do this?

He'd made his decision, but it was still hard to say it out loud. "Okay."

Charli's beautiful blue eyes widened, almost as if she was surprised by his answer. Had she thought he was going to refuse her?

"You'll marry me?"

He nodded. "This is the best thing for Levi. And for you."

Her face took on a pained expression. "But not for you?"

"This isn't really about me, but I've thought it through, and I'm good with it."

"Okay, then," Charli said, though she still didn't look completely certain. Was she second-guessing her own idea...?

A *Publishers Weekly* bestselling and award-winning author of over forty novels, with almost two million books in print, **Deb Kastner** enjoys writing contemporary inspirational Western stories set in small communities. Deb lives in beautiful Colorado with her husband, miscreant mutts and curious kitties. She is blessed with three adult daughters and two grandchildren. Her favorite hobby is spoiling her grandchildren, but she also enjoys reading, watching movies, listening to music—The Texas Tenors are her favorite—singing in the church choir and exploring the Rocky Mountains on horseback.

Books by Deb Kastner

Love Inspired

Big Sky Legacy

The Surprise Cowboy Dad

K-9 Companions

Bonding with the Babies

Rocky Mountain Family

The Black Sheep's Salvation
Opening Her Heart
The Marine's Mission
Their Unbreakable Bond
A Reason to Stay

Visit the Author Profile page at LoveInspired.com for more titles.

THE SURPRISE COWBOY DAD

DEB KASTNER

LOVE INSPIRED
INSPIRATIONAL ROMANCE

If you purchased this book without a cover you should be aware that this book is stolen property. It was reported as "unsold and destroyed" to the publisher, and neither the author nor the publisher has received any payment for this "stripped book."

MIX
Paper | Supporting responsible forestry
FSC® C021394

ISBN-13: 978-1-335-62159-7

Recycling programs for this product may not exist in your area.

The Surprise Cowboy Dad

Copyright © 2026 by Debra Kastner

All rights reserved. No part of this book may be used or reproduced in any manner whatsoever without written permission.

Without limiting the exclusive rights of any author, contributor or the publisher of this publication, any unauthorized use of this publication to train generative artificial intelligence (AI) technologies is expressly prohibited. Harlequin also exercises their rights under Article 4(3) of the Digital Single Market Directive 2019/790 and expressly reserves this publication from the text and data mining exception.

This is a work of fiction. Names, characters, places and incidents are either the product of the author's imagination or are used fictitiously. Any resemblance to actual persons, living or dead, businesses, companies, events or locales is entirely coincidental.

For questions and comments about the quality of this book, please contact us at CustomerService@Harlequin.com.

® is a trademark of Harlequin Enterprises ULC.

Love Inspired
22 Adelaide St. West, 41st Floor
Toronto, Ontario M5H 4E3, Canada
www.LoveInspired.com

HarperCollins Publishers
Macken House, 39/40 Mayor Street Upper,
Dublin 1, D01 C9W8, Ireland
www.HarperCollins.com

Printed in Lithuania

Surely he hath borne our griefs,
and carried our sorrows: yet we did esteem him stricken,
smitten of God, and afflicted.
—*Isaiah* 53:4

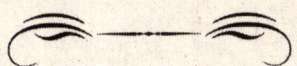

I lost my father during the writing of this book, so my heart feels for heroine Charli in her grief. My dad was the first person to introduce me to books and his own love of reading. This one is for you, Dad. Give Jesus a hug for me.

Chapter One

You can't be serious.

Charlotte Stafford—Charli to her friends—cringed inwardly as her mother's sharp, stabbing words echoed in her head.

Oddly enough, Charli's own thoughts were a repeat of what Martha's words had been. She hardly even thought of the woman who'd biologically given birth to her as Mom anymore, but *Martha*. It had been so many years since they'd had any kind of family relationship. They hadn't even spoken on the phone in such a long time. At first it had been birthdays and Christmas, but as the years had gone on, they'd spoken less and less.

And now the woman wanted to force her to sell the ranch?

You can't be serious, Mom.

She'd never give up her ranch. Not in this lifetime.

She remembered how her mom's bitter voice over the phone line had continued, explaining her case. Charli had squeezed her cell phone to her ear and gritted her teeth.

It's not fair to your sisters for you to retain the family property. We've all read the will and know what it says. It's obviously not what your father wanted. And anyway, you can't do this alone even if you wanted to.

By her words *do this alone*, her mother meant her ability to single-handedly run the Hope, Montana, ranch on which Charli had grown up and spent the happiest years of her life with her father.

Her mother hadn't been here. How would she know what Charli was capable of?

She couldn't believe her father was gone. And in a twist that had surprised them all, his will had equally divided his assets between her and her two sisters with extra in a trust for her mom.

Her mother and two sisters had just arrived in Montana. It was three against one. Charli wasn't ready, and she felt completely alone.

What kind of fresh nightmare was this?

As she always did when she needed to think, Charli saddled up her favorite sleek gray Arab gelding—Sir Percy Blakeney, or Percy for short—and led him out of the barn. As soon as she mounted, she gave him his head, leaning into his gallop, the beat of his hooves matching that of her heart. Percy was an expert horsewoman's mount, and she adored riding him both on her best days and her worst days. Today was no different.

Without realizing she was doing so, she rode across her land until she spotted the big green tractor parked in the middle of one of the far fields. Cows crowded nearby.

Of course.

She'd subconsciously been looking for Henry Parker. He'd been her father's only ranch hand for years, and she'd known him her whole life. She didn't need to give him all the details on what was happening now. He already knew her family's whole history—that she and her mother and siblings were at odds with each other and had been for many years. That she hadn't communicated with that part of her family because of the rift between her mom and dad. Henry would listen to her vent without judging her or thinking the worst of her for the way she was feeling. No doubt he'd even agree she'd been put in an untenable position.

She turned Percy toward the tractor and trotted down the mild slope, reining him in before Henry, who was spreading a bale of hay for the cattle.

He looked up, his lips curling into a smile as he respectfully tipped his black cowboy hat with his thumb and forefinger.

Charli dismounted and ran a hand over her long blond hair, tightening her ponytail against her windswept appearance.

"Out for a ride?" he asked, his dark eyebrows rising.

She sighed. "You could say that."

As in *the ride of her life*. What a roller coaster.

She was momentarily distracted by Henry's dog, a Kelpie named Red, who was running along the outside of the cattle, gathering up any wandering cows and herding them back toward Henry. The dog worked instinctively and didn't even need any instruction or attention to do his job.

All of a sudden, Charli felt a nipping sensation at her heel, something biting at her cowboy boots. She looked down to see the most adorable Kelpie puppy ever, growling playfully as he pulled on the hem of her jeans. She immediately snatched him up and cuddled him in her arms, tucking him underneath her chin as she scratched behind his ears.

"Who is this?" she asked, feeling her heart lighten

just a little as the puppy wiggled his whole backside and licked her chin.

"Little Blue," Henry replied. "Got him today. I was at the hardware store earlier and they had a box with three puppies behind the counter. I didn't go in with the intention of coming out with a puppy, but Blue picked me out. He hopped out of the box on his own and scratched my jeans until I paid attention to him. I thought we could use the extra help with our expanding herd, and I figured with Red showing him the ropes, it won't take much to train him up."

She could imagine just how it had happened. He had such a big heart. Charli almost teased Henry about his choice of names. What a guy thing—*Red* and *Blue*. Except she could immediately see just why Henry had gone with the moniker he had, and it wasn't because his full-grown Kelpie was named Red. Or at least, that wasn't the whole reason. Little Blue had striking blue eyes.

Even though Little Blue was a working dog, Charli continued to hold him, stroking his neck and taking comfort from his wiggly, furry form.

Henry narrowed his gaze on her. "What's wrong?"

As usual, Henry was completely attuned to her. He always seemed to automatically know what she was thinking and feeling, something she appreciated about their friendship. He was so much more than just an employee on her father's ranch.

Her ranch, now. And no matter what her family threw at her, she was going to fight tooth and nail to make sure it stayed that way.

"Who said anything was wrong?" She tried for light

banter, but it fell completely flat, and she knew it. And from the look on Henry's face, he knew it, too.

He raised both dark eyebrows, his bright blue eyes intense, and leaned his muscular forearm on the pitchfork he'd been using to spread the hay. The pulse throbbing at the edge of his square jaw and his silence was more telling than any words he could have said.

"You know my mom and sisters are in town. I just found out why based on what's in my father's will," Charli finally admitted. "What a mess."

Henry's expression went from raised eyebrows to furrowed ones. "How so?"

"I never thought he would do this, but I just found out Dad split everything he owned equally between the three of us girls." She could hardly believe it even now as she said the words aloud.

"What?" Henry vigorously shook his head. "No way. There must be some kind of mistake. You and your dad were like this." He twisted his pointer and middle fingers together. "He raised you as a single father. He wouldn't give the ranch to anyone other than you and only you."

"Yeah? Well, apparently, he did. I'm having a hard time believing it myself," she snapped, then took a deep breath. "Sorry. I don't mean to be taking out my frustrations on you. I've been thinking about why this happened. I always assumed I would inherit from Dad, and Fiona and Cordelia would inherit from Mom. That's what made the most sense to me. But as near as I can figure, Dad had this crazy dying wish that my sisters and my mom and I would all reconcile when we split this inheritance.

"Why he thought it would or even should happen now, when he never tried to reunite us all in his lifetime, is beyond me. But he's put me in an impossible, heartbreaking position. And as if that isn't bad enough, Mom is being really pushy to get this all tied up. She's adamant that I can't run the ranch all on my own, even though she doesn't know anything about me. She certainly won't listen to anything I have to say to the contrary."

"You aren't on your own," he said quietly. "I mean, you have me at your side, for what it's worth."

"And I appreciate that. I really do." The puppy started wiggling in earnest and she let him down. He immediately started barking and bounded to Red's side to imitate the older dog herding the cattle, while Red mostly ignored the younger Kelpie.

Charli flopped to the earth cross-legged, pressing her palms to her dry but aching eyes. "I haven't been able to cry since my father passed. Not at all. And now this, and I still can't find it within myself to grieve. I don't know, Henry. I think something's wrong with me."

"No." Henry dropped the pitchfork and came up behind her, dropping to his knees and wrapping his thick, comforting arms around her, pressing his hand to her cheek and pulling her head into his chest until she could hear the steady thrum of his heartbeat. For a long moment he gently rocked her. He didn't try to fill the space with words, for there wasn't anything to say.

After some time, she pulled away from him and rolled to her feet, sniffling even though she still hadn't shed a tear. Henry followed, standing beside her with his hands tucked into the front pockets of his jeans and concern flooding from his gaze.

"What are you going to do?" he asked at last.

"I have no earthly idea. But what I'm *not* going to do

is give up this ranch. It's my home. If my mom thinks otherwise, she has another thing coming." She pulled out her cell phone and checked the time. "Martha and my sisters are waiting for me back at the house," she said with a sigh. "I guess it's not going to do me any good to keep avoiding the situation. Or rather, avoiding my mom and sisters, as much as I'd like to."

"Anything I can do?"

She stared at him for a moment. There was something, but she knew it was a big ask, especially for someone like Henry, a quiet, nonconfrontational man.

"I know you're busy and it's asking a lot of you, but would you mind coming with me to back me up? I have no idea what to expect, but whatever it is can't be good. I've spoken to Martha on the phone from time to time, though not often, but I haven't seen her or my sisters in twenty years."

Twenty years of heartbreak and irreconcilable differences. How could her father possibly expect her to fix things now?

"Of course I'll back you up." Henry wanted to reach out and touch her arm, but he restrained himself, keeping his hands in his pockets. He'd already overstepped his boundaries today. He'd do well to remember that he was Charli's ranch hand, her employee, even though they worked together side by side. At the end of the day, she was his boss, not his friend, although right now it kind of felt as if she was asking for his support as one. In any case, he would always have her back, no matter what, whether she knew it or not. On his side, he was her tried and true friend and always would be.

Hadn't she helped him in more ways than he could count over the years? If it weren't for her, he'd still be reading and writing at an elementary school level and would never have been able to get his GED.

Remembering the effects of his dyslexia and dysgraphia still embarrassed him. From the time he was in kindergarten, he knew he was different, and it hadn't been long before other kids had caught on and teased him. It wasn't long before he'd become a loner.

Charli had never treated him as *less than* in any way. Nor had her father, John, who'd believed in him and given him a job at the Stafford ranch when no one else would give him the time of day. He'd been terribly bullied as a child and still felt like a dunce around most people, which he supposed was why he enjoyed working with horses, cattle and dogs so much. Animals didn't judge a man for how well he did academically.

And neither did Charli.

"I'll finish taking care of the cattle and get back to the house as quick as I can," he said, whistling the dogs back to his side before scooping Little Blue into his hand and crawling up onto the tractor. "This old thing can't go nearly as fast as Percy, though, so it may be a few minutes more."

"I don't want to go in without you, so I'll walk Percy back and rub him down. That way you'll have time to catch up. Meet me in the barn and we'll walk up to the ranch house together, okay?"

"Yep," Henry replied, setting the puppy on his lap and cranking the engine. Red followed along beside the tractor.

Charli was already waiting outside for him when he

pulled up next to the barn and shut off the tractor. He glanced at her under the shadow of the brim of his hat as he put the dogs in the nearby kennel and tried to judge her state of mind. She looked as if she was getting ready to enter a fiery dragon's lair, which, he supposed, in a way, she was.

"Ready?" he asked.

"No," she said, her voice unsteady. "Not in the least. But it's not going to get any easier if I wait. Thanks for coming in with me."

"Not a problem."

Charli took a deep breath, straightened her shoulders, lifted her chin and marched toward the ranch house, Henry lagging just behind her. His body was tensing the closer they got to the house, so he couldn't even begin to imagine how she felt.

There were two vehicles he didn't recognize parked in front of the house, one a smaller-sized blue SUV and one a black sedan, which he assumed belonged to or had been rented by Charli's mom and sisters.

When they entered the house, the sound of women chatting immediately ceased, leaving such an uncomfortable silence it almost felt like it was echoing.

"Charli?" It was an older woman's rich alto voice. Martha Stafford, Charli's mom, Henry guessed, though he hadn't seen her since he was a kid. "We're all waiting in the family room. Thanks for leaving the door unlocked for us."

"No problem. I wasn't sure how long I'd be, and I didn't want you all to be stuck outside," Charli replied, her voice tight. "That's the nature of ranch work."

"I remember," Martha called back. "Oh, so well."

She didn't sound thrilled about the memory.

Charli slid off her boots and entered the kitchen from the mud room. Henry followed, again lagging a bit, not because he didn't want to support Charli but because this was her family, and he didn't know how they were going to feel about his involvement.

Martha was more or less the way Henry remembered, although of course she'd aged—in a good way, Henry thought. She'd once worn her hair shoulder length, but now she'd colored her bob a dark reddish brown and still had fine facial features with distinctly high cheekbones and a long, slender jawline.

On the other hand, Henry wouldn't have recognized Charli's sisters if he'd walked by them on the street. Thinking back, they'd all been small children when Fiona and Cordelia had moved away from Hope. They'd both grown into lovely women, and all three sisters were quite distinct from each other. Fiona was a tiny sprite of a woman with copper penny hair and green eyes, while Cordelia was more full-figured with brown hair and blue eyes. Both were quite attractive in their own ways, although nothing like Charli.

Henry wasn't great at reading a room, but he could read Charli. When Fiona stood, leaped forward and wrapped her arms around Charli with a squeal, Charli stood stiff and unmoving, her arms at her sides and her hands in fists. He knew her reddening cheeks had nothing to do with embarrassment. Anger, more likely, and frustration.

Fiona didn't appear to notice her sister's reaction. "It's been too long!" she exclaimed, giving Charli a teeth-chattering shake. "We're so happy to be here."

Were they really?

And suddenly it was too long? As far as Henry knew, Charli and her sisters hadn't even spoken, much less seen each other, since Martha and John divorced. *Too long* didn't begin to cover it, and it wasn't as if the reconciliation was mutual.

Henry glanced around at the other faces and decided Fiona was the only one who felt positively about this awkward family reunion. Henry was aware of the backstory—the family had split when John and Martha had divorced. Martha and the younger two girls had moved to a Denver suburb, and as far as he knew, not one of them had been back to Hope since, much less visited the ranch. He didn't even know if Charli had had any communication with them at all through the years.

He doubted it. She'd always been fiercely loyal to her father, who'd never spoken of her sisters, at least not to Henry.

"We need to sit down and have a serious conversation," Martha said without preamble. "The immediate family, that is." She narrowed her eyes upon Henry. "Will you excuse us, please, Henry?"

Charli set her jaw and crossed her arms. "Anything you can say to me, you can say to Henry. He stays."

As much as he wanted to be here to support Charli, he was beginning to wish he hadn't agreed to come. If the daggers shooting out of Martha's eyes were anything to go by, he might just be making matters worse for Charli rather than offering her the support she so clearly needed.

They gathered in the family room, her sisters sitting comfortably on the sofa while Martha sat looking not quite at ease on an old-fashioned armchair. Charli perched, her back ramrod straight and her breath coming quickly, on a leather ottoman, clutching her straw cowboy hat in her hands and rolling the brim so tightly he wasn't sure it would last beyond the afternoon.

Rather than sitting in the easy chair that matched the ottoman, Henry stood behind her, crossing his arms and rocking back on his heels as he physically absorbed the stress running through Charli. He hoped she could feel the strength he was trying to offer. He imagined how she must feel being ganged up on this way—three-on-one, or actually, four-on-one in a way, since her beloved father had ostensibly written his will to be pitted against her.

How could he have left her this way? John had been such a good man. Hadn't he considered Charli's feelings?

"I have spoken to your father's lawyer, Benjamin Adams," Martha started, running her hand across a file folder of information she'd tucked onto her lap. "We'll be meeting with him in a couple of days to do the formal reading of the will and to clarify and answer questions you may have, but since this is a special situation, I wanted to meet with you all first."

"Why?"

Henry wasn't surprised when Charli spoke up, though perhaps he was startled by how quickly she responded.

Martha met Charli's gaze straight on. "That's a reasonable question. There are things I believe we need to discuss as a family before we get to the technical reading of the will." She opened the folder and removed three sealed envelopes. Charli's name was scribbled on the first one in what Henry immediately recognized as John's large cursive script. The other two were addressed to Fiona and Cordelia. "These letters should answer most of your questions."

"And how do you know that? Have you read the letters?" Charli asked, her voice tight.

"No. I got a letter, too, one that was addressed to me. That's why I understand John's wishes in all this and why I insisted we all meet up here in Hope at the ranch. John specifically asked me to work with Ben in the execution of his will because he wants me to facilitate getting us all together again after all these years. He…wants us to be open to reconciliation."

"And he thought suggesting this brilliant idea in his will was going to change everything?" Cordelia said with a scoff. "Only after he's passed on and can't face us himself. I can't even believe he thinks we'll just join hands and sing 'Kumbaya' because he says to. If you ask me, waiting until after his death makes him a coward."

Charli stiffened, and Henry laid a hand on her shoulder, half afraid she was going to jump at her sister's throat. He was half tempted to do the same. How dare she suggest John was anything but honorable?

"Daddy was *not* a coward," Charli said, the words bit off. "He was the bravest man I've ever known, and you have no right to speak of him that way."

Cordelia wasn't backing down. "A man who never once visited his own daughters after the divorce. Not in all these years. And suddenly he wants us to be a family again?"

Martha held up her hands to stop the bickering between them. "Please don't blame your father for that. I am equally to blame for our estrangement and for the way we chose to do things. John and I made a mutual decision when we split our family to make it a clean cut and not have divided families where the children were always being lobbed between parents on weekends and holidays. We decided Charli would be happiest staying with her father on the ranch, while I took the younger children with me. Right or wrong, that's how it happened. And I'm here now trying to work things out because like John, I feel responsible for the outcome. I now realize it was wrong of us to keep you all apart, and I hope each of you will grow to know and love your sisters."

A long, tense silence lit the room, making Henry itch to return to the open air where he felt comfortable and could actually breathe.

"Charli, I need to speak with you alone, please." Martha dismissed her other daughters with a wave and then, after Fiona and Cordelia left the room, leveled her gaze on Henry. "Alone," she repeated.

Charli leaned a palm back on the ottoman and met Henry's gaze. "It's okay. I'll meet you outside when we're finished."

Henry wasn't at all sure it was *okay*, or even that Charli was okay, but he replaced his hat and tipped it to both ladies before leaving the room.

"I don't know what your father ever saw in that boy," he heard Martha say after he'd entered the mudroom to put his boots back on. "He's a high school dropout with very little to offer the world." Henry's shoulders immediately stiffened into knots, and he froze with his foot halfway into one of his boots.

"Mom," Charli protested. "Stop. Henry is a hard worker here on the ranch, and he's wonderful with the animals. That's why Daddy hired him. He's an excellent ranch hand. Besides, he went back and got his GED. That shows real commitment and I'm proud of him."

Henry could practically picture Martha's chin rise as she sniffed in disdain, though in truth maybe he wasn't being fair. He couldn't tell what her expression held from where he was standing. "I understand that John made decisions he thought were best for the ranch, and for whatever reason, that included hiring Henry. And maybe he has done good work for you. But keep in mind that sooner or later that young man will be looking for a new job. He'll want a family of his own, and no doubt his own ranch. By then, Lord willing, you'll be far away from here, hopefully making a *real* life for yourself."

Henry thrust his feet into his boots and stomped out the door. Martha had jabbed a knife right into the worst of his own insecurities by speaking of his lack of education and lack of worth, but that wasn't what bothered him the most.

It was the idea that Charli might be going away.

Chapter Two

"Mom, I'm not going to let you talk about Henry that way," Charli protested, leaning toward Martha. "And as I said on the phone, you can forget about me leaving this ranch. I grew up here, and I intend to stay and make my life here. It's my home, now and always. It's where I belong, and I'll fight tooth and nail to keep it. We'll just have to figure out some other way to fairly split up Daddy's legacy, one that doesn't involve selling this ranch because I'm not leaving."

"But you're an educated young woman with so much potential," Martha argued, the frown that followed accentuating her high cheekbones. "I don't know how much influence your father had on you, but I suspect your current emotions may have to do with him. He felt the same way about this ranch. Just look at yourself. You could have gone to an Ivy League college, but instead, for reasons I'll never understand, you chose to go to a local university. You have a business degree you're not even using."

Charli chuckled dryly. "My degree is in agribusiness, Mom. And I'm using it every single day—right here on the ranch."

Martha sighed. "Perhaps you should read your father's

letter. Maybe then you won't want to argue with me anymore."

Charli's hands shook as she dropped her gaze to the sealed envelope on her lap, the one with the bold script she had immediately recognized as being her father's.

Oh, how she missed him. Her throat tightened with raw emotion.

Taking a deep breath, she slid a finger under the seal and pulled a single page from inside, carefully unfolding it.

My Dear, Sweet Charli,
I know how difficult this must be for you to understand. You've always owned my heart, ever since you were a little girl. But I need to ask your forgiveness in this one thing. I should never have kept you from your sisters and mother. It's my one regret, and one I pray I can still resolve. I hope I am not too little, too late.

I ask you now to dig deep down into your heart and welcome them to the ranch and into your life with open arms.

I know how much you love this ranch. Trust me when I say that in the end, I truly believe love will find a way.
God be with you.
Daddy

Her chest ached as if a fist was squeezing until her heart could no longer beat, but still there were no tears. Why could she not grieve like a normal human being? But perhaps it was better this way. She didn't want to cry right now, not in front of her mother. She needed to be strong.

Martha sat straight-backed, her lips pursed as she silently watched Charli and waited for her to finish reading. Charli looked up, then handed her the letter without a word.

Her mother glanced over it, then nodded, folded the note and handed it back to her. Charli waited for her to give her opinion, but her mother remained silent.

"Daddy wants me to keep the ranch," Charli said at last.

"That's not exactly what the letter says," Martha protested.

"Yes, it does. Maybe not in so many words, but he knew how much this ranch means to me. There's nowhere else I want to be, and I won't be happy anywhere else."

"And your sisters? What about them?"

"Honestly, I don't know. I need to look at Daddy's assets and crunch some numbers. Maybe we can work out some kind of solution where I give part of my annual cattle sales to each of them."

"You'll sell off your stock?"

"I can't sell any more than I usually do. I don't know if you remember how a cow/calf operation works. I've got my permanent herd of cows, and then each year I sell off the calves those ladies produce. My production varies from year to year, but God has blessed us. We've been fruitful over the past few years, and the ranch is stable."

"I understand perfectly. And I do remember how it works. I grew up in this town, remember? I married a rancher. I even lived on this exact ranch for many years. Which is why I have to question why you believe you can do this all on your own. Because I honestly don't think you can. I'm not trying to be mean. Just realistic."

Her mother's blatant disbelief stung deep, maybe because what she was saying was one of Charli's deepest fears. She couldn't let Martha see that, though. She had to steer the conversation in the right direction.

"I am being realistic. Daddy and I successfully ran the ranch ourselves all these years, and he taught me everything I know. Like we talked about, I went to college. And of course, I have Henry here to help me. He knows the ranch as well as I do."

"Don't forget that boy could decide to walk out any time he wants."

"Stop calling him *that boy*. Henry is a full-grown man, and he is the most honorable, hardworking guy I know."

"I don't trust him."

"I didn't ask you to," she snapped. This conversation was going nowhere. No matter how much she trusted Henry, there was no way to prove to her mother that he wasn't going to take off and desert her and the ranch, nor could she think of a way for Mom to see that she was capable of managing the place herself even if Henry left.

Charli's cell phone buzzed in the back pocket of her jeans, and she fished it out. Henry's name flashed on the screen. She couldn't imagine why he was calling. Probably to check up on her. But it gave her an excuse to remove herself from this fruitless conversation.

"I'm sorry. I've got to take this," she told Martha and then walked out to the mudroom to escape her mother's presence.

"Hey, Henry," she said as she picked up. "Thanks for calling and giving me a way out of this nightmare. I'm just finishing up with Mom. You won't believe—"

"Charli." Henry cut her off mid-sentence. "I—I need you to come out here right away. I didn't know who else to call."

There was a note of genuine panic in his tone, which was totally unlike him. Henry never got worked up about anything. He was the calmest person she knew. How many times had she seen him gently coaxing a sick newborn calf through a rough time or working with a stubborn horse with the utmost patience and care?

"Sure," she agreed immediately. "Where are you?"

"At my cabin. I—I just… Please. Get here as fast as you can!"

He'd been living in a small cabin on the Stafford land for many years now as it was convenient for everyone involved. He had a roof over his head, and she and her father had someone they could call in a pinch no matter what the issue.

Now it was her turn to be there for him.

"I'm on my way," she assured him. "Henry? Henry?"

He'd already cut the call.

Henry stood in the middle of the kitchen trying to steady his breath as pure, unbridled panic roared through his veins. His heart hammered in his chest and pounded up into his throat. He hoped Charli would hurry. Maybe she would know what to do, because he had no idea. He couldn't believe this was happening.

Oh, Jamie Lynn.

What had his sister been thinking? She must be using again. She'd struggled with addiction from the time she was in junior high. But she'd told him she was better now, and he'd had no reason to doubt her.

Clearly, though, she'd been lying. It was the only explanation that made any sense to him. Nothing—*nothing*—could justify what he was seeing before him.

"Henry?" Charli's concerned voice came from just outside the door. She didn't bother knocking or waiting but let herself in. "What's up? You sounded so worried on the phone."

"I'm in here," he called. "The kitchen."

"I hurried over as fast as I—" Her voice came to an abrupt halt and she skidded to a stop, her boots sliding across the wooden floor. She breathed out audibly. "Whoa."

"Yeah," Henry agreed, his voice hoarse. "*Whoa* is right."

"Who is this?" Tentatively, she approached the four-month-old baby still strapped into his car seat. The infant had been safely placed on the floor next to the kitchen table and was staring back at them with large blue eyes that were full of curiosity. Charli reached out to him and smiled as the baby wrapped a chubby fist around her thumb.

"If I had to guess, I would say he's my sister's baby, Levi," Henry said, his voice gruff with emotion. "I've never seen him before today. She disappears for months and sometimes years at a time when she's using."

Charli regarded the baby for a moment. "What a cutie. I can see where he'd be related. He looks like you, with that black tuft of hair and those big blue eyes."

He nodded. "I guess so."

"Where did you find him? Did you talk to Jamie Lynn? I didn't see her."

He shook his head. "Neither did I. I got hungry while I was waiting for you to finish talking to your mom, so I came back to the cabin to grab a sandwich for dinner before I went back to the ranch house to meet up with you. I walked in, and there he was. Thankfully, when I got here he was sleeping and not crying, or else I really don't know what I would have done. As it is..." He left the rest of his sentence hanging.

"And your sister is...where?"

"That I do not know." He moved his hands from his hips and crossed his arms over his chest, feeling defensive and completely off-kilter. "You know she's never been a very responsible individual at the best of times and worse when she's using, but I can't imagine what she was thinking leaving her baby here at the cabin all by himself. What if I hadn't come in when I did? What if I was out of town and the baby would have been left here for an extended period of time?" He shoved his hands back through his hair and growled in frustration.

"Did you check your phone to see if she tried to leave you a message? Or try to call her?"

He shook his head and wordlessly handed her his phone. In his panic, the only person he'd thought to call was Charli, and it only took her a quick glance at his phone to confirm that Henry had neither called nor received a call or text from Jamie Lynn.

"I'm too angry to confront her right now," he confessed, his face warming. "I know I'll have to reach out to her at some point, but I'm not going to be able to hold in my anger."

She reached for his hand and gave it a reassuring squeeze. "You have every right to feel that way. Give yourself some time to process your emotions."

The baby, who up until this point had been calm, suddenly wailed in distress. Adrenaline coursed through

Henry at the sound. It was foreign noise, and he felt so helpless. What was he supposed to do now?

"I guess we ought to get this little guy out of his car seat," Charli said, unhooking the straps and lifting Levi into her arms. Levi immediately stopped crying. To his knowledge, she had no more experience with infants than he had, yet she sounded completely calm and collected, whereas the hair on Henry's arms was standing on end. His nerves were zapping like electrodes, and he wanted to bolt.

"We'll figure out what to do about Jamie Lynn later," she continued. "I suspect the first order of business is a diaper change. I know less than nothing about babies, but that makes sense. What do you think, little man?" She stared at Levi a moment longer. "You know, I don't even think I've ever held a baby before." She paused thoughtfully. "Have you checked the diaper bag yet to see if your sister left us any supplies?"

"You'd never know this is your first time with a baby. You're a natural."

Charli threw him a glance and snorted. "Yeah, right."

Maybe she didn't know more than he did, but Henry hadn't even thought about looking for a diaper bag, much less noticed the bag sitting on a kitchen chair. He'd been so worried—paralyzed, really—that he hadn't taken his eyes off the baby since he'd first arrived at his cabin.

"Okay," he said, unzipping the bag. "What am I looking for? Just a diaper?"

He hated that he was displaying his ignorance again, but he'd literally never been around a baby before in his life, much less changed one. He supposed he and Charli would have to work it out together. People changed diapers on thousands of babies every day. How hard could it really be?

"What do we even need? A diaper and probably a package of wipes," Charli suggested. "Diaper rash cream? I really have no clue." She kissed the baby on his chubby cheek and then blew a raspberry on his belly. "We'll get you clean and dry and then see what we can do about getting a bottle made up for you," she cooed to Levi in the high voice adults tended to use with babies.

"That makes sense," Henry agreed. "I have no idea what to do. I hope you're better than I am at changing a diaper because I expect I'm going to be awful at it. Mixing up a bottle of milk and feeding it to him, maybe not so much, since I've done it with the calves."

She chuckled. "No excuses. Levi is your nephew, and diaper changes go with the territory. But how hard can it really be to change a baby?"

"I was just thinking the same thing. Or at least I'm trying to convince myself of that."

As Henry located a diaper and a package of wipes, he noticed a crumpled sheet of paper that looked as if it had been torn from a spiral notebook and balled up, then shoved into the bag. He handed the diaper to Charli and unfolded the note, scanning the contents with a dark frown before clearing his throat. He hated reading aloud, but Charli needed to hear this—now. He began speaking in a shaky voice.

"'I'm sorry. I can't do this, and Levi's real father isn't and never has been part of the picture. I have to do what's best for the baby, and I trust you to do what is right. I've left all his legal documents in a folder in the baby bag with the hope that you'll adopt him. I've always looked up to you and know you'll make Levi a great father. Please, Henry. Love him as you would your own son.'"

He dropped his hand to his side and the paper fluttered to the floor. Charli met his gaze, her mouth gaping wide.

"You have got to be kidding me. She just abandoned her kid? Left you her baby without so much as talking to you about it?" she asked in astonishment. "Who *does* that?"

"My sister, evidently." Henry's blood pounded in his brain, and he pressed his fingers to his temples against the headache that was quickly developing. In an instant, he broke into a cold sweat. The gravity of what was happening suddenly weighed down on him. "I can't take care of a baby, much less raise one. I wouldn't even know where to start."

"I know you aren't on speaking terms with your mom and dad, so they probably aren't going to help you, but maybe you could appeal to their instincts as grandparents?"

Levi shook his head. "They cut both Jamie Lynn and me out of their lives. They travel so much I don't even know where they are."

"I'm sorry to have brought it up," Charli said.

"Not your fault," Henry said.

"I was just wondering if there is anyone else you can call to take him? Extended family? An aunt, uncle or cousin, maybe?"

Henry shook his head. "My sister and I are the only Parkers left in our family besides my folks. Well, and now baby Levi."

"So it's just you. If that's the case, I'm not sure what your options are." With a now comfortable and dry baby,

Charli rummaged through the diaper bag and pulled out a bottle and a can of powdered formula. She seemed to have no problem doing it all one-handed, as if she'd been taking care of a baby all her life. "You can call social services, I guess. Maybe that would be the best thing for you to do. I know we don't talk about this much because it's a painful topic, but I know your sister has struggled with drug addictions and making good decisions in the past. She's not making good decisions for herself now if she just leaves her son alone in your cabin. Clearly, she's still experiencing difficulties."

He watched as she mixed the formula, settled herself on a chair and started feeding Levi. For some reason watching Charli and Levi comforted him. Henry had bottle-fed dozens of calves over the years. How different could a human baby be?

"Would social services put him in foster care?" he wondered aloud.

"Maybe." She sounded uncertain. "I assume that's what they'd do if they put Levi in the system."

"No. I'm not going to do that to Levi." Henry's decision was made in an instant, but his heart confirmed what he already knew to be true. Levi was his flesh and blood, and he wouldn't allow the baby to be taken away by anyone. Even though this was the first time he'd ever laid eyes on the infant, he already had more love in his heart for the child than he could have imagined. "This baby is my family and my responsibility. I will seek legal guardianship and raise him as my own son."

"I understand how you feel. It's the kind of man you are. But it's a lot to take in all at once. You don't have to figure out everything right this second. Maybe you should give it some time and think about it before you make a permanent decision as to his care."

Henry vigorously shook his head. "There's nothing to think about. Levi is my nephew. If my sister can't take care of him, then I will. End of subject."

"I admire you for that," she said softly, holding the baby on her shoulder and patting his tiny back. "I'm sure that's why Jamie Lynn did what she did."

"I don't know about that. She was clearly not thinking straight when she dropped him off here. It scares me to think she was driving with a baby in the car."

"Or driving at all, for that matter," Charli added with a nod of agreement. "Even without Levi in the car, it appears she's a danger to herself and others." She took a deep breath. "Okay, so what are you going to do here, practically speaking? You need some kind of plan. It looks as if Jamie Lynn provided enough in the way of diapers and formula to get you through the first couple of days, but if you're really set on doing this, you'll need to shop for some baby stuff and get a nursery set up."

Henry blanched, feeling as if he'd been run over by a herd of cattle and trampled to the earth by their hooves. "I don't even know where to start."

"I don't either, but I'm willing to help. How about we go out tomorrow and do some serious baby item shopping?"

Henry hated shopping almost as much as he loved ranching, but she was right, and he didn't see a way out of it. He needed stuff for Levi. And maybe, between the two of them, they could kinda-sorta figure out all the *stuff* Levi was going to need to get by.

Charli held out the baby for Henry to take. He gritted

his teeth as he put his palms under the baby's shoulders, feeling awkward and afraid he was either going to crush the poor little mite with his large hands or drop him. He held the baby out at arm's length and dangled him there.

Charli laughed. "Just put him up against your shoulder and try to relax. He's sturdier than you'd expect. Gently pat his back and see if you can get a good burp out of him. Where's your laptop?"

"It's on my nightstand," Henry answered. He watched as Charli brought his laptop from his bedroom and sat down at the table, opening the computer and booting it up. She pulled her legs up, crossing them as she leaned forward and typed into the search engine.

Henry stood behind her, looking over her shoulder as he held Levi and mimicking what he'd seen Charli do, surprised when it started feeling more comforting than awkward. He found himself swaying without even thinking about it. "It's okay, little guy," he whispered. "Uncle Henry is here."

"Here's the state website for legal guardianship. I'll save the forms and send them to my work email, and then we can fill them out and print them off at my office in the ranch house. It's probably something we need to do sooner rather than later."

He was musing over how much he appreciated Charli's support when a thought occurred to him that felt like a kick behind the knees. It would have dropped him like a rock if he hadn't been holding the baby. As it was, his stomach instantly knotted.

"I'm a guy," he said with a frown.

"What?" Charli was clearly confused, raising her eyebrows and looking up at him as if he'd lost all his marbles.

Maybe he had. "I'm a guy," he repeated.

"Okay, my first reaction to that statement is, '*Well, duh*,' but somehow I don't think you're just trying to state the obvious," Charli said with a chuckle.

"No. I mean, obviously I'm a guy. What I'm trying to say is that the court system doesn't usually favor single men in guardianship situations, do they? Don't they want something more stable?"

Charli twisted her lips as she thought it through. "I honestly don't know the answer to that question. But there isn't anyone else, right? The father isn't in the picture, and you're the closest blood relative who is willing to step up and do the right thing. Surely they'll give you guardianship over putting the poor baby in the system if they don't have to, won't they?"

He ran his palm across his jaw, scratching his scruff. He'd never been so terrified in his life, not even during the four days he'd taken the tests for his GED.

He suddenly had a colossal fight ahead of him that hadn't even been on his radar an hour ago. The old saying that life could change in the blink of an eye couldn't have been more accurate at this moment.

What was he going to do with a baby?

Chapter Three

Charli had stayed late at the cabin with a very anxious Henry that Friday night, working out everything she thought he'd need to know about taking care of Levi—at least enough to get him through the night on his own, and she'd promised to return to help him the first thing in the morning. Dawn had found them both bleary eyed from lack of sleep, Henry because he'd been up taking care of the baby all night, and Charli because she hadn't been able to get her mind to shut down as she considered and discarded possibility after possibility regarding their dilemmas—how she was going to be able to keep her ranch and how Henry would be able to adapt to his new role as guardian to an infant. Unable to sleep, she'd opened her laptop and searched online, making a list of everything she thought Henry and Levi would need to get through the first few months together.

While they'd planned on shopping for the baby, there was ranch work to be done before they could go. Ranchers didn't get days off, not even when their whole lives were in sudden turmoil. So Charli had watched Levi while Henry did the necessary chores. Then they'd headed out to Great Falls to do their shopping, baby in tow. Despite her fatigue and stress, Charli enjoyed the excursion, and she didn't miss the many smiles sent in their direction by strangers who probably thought she, Henry and Levi were a young family. The thought made her smile. If they really had been a family, they would have been a cute trio.

The next day was Sunday, and Henry had voiced to Charli that he was worried about taking Levi to church, so once again she had stepped in to help. Their church was welcoming to children of all ages and was always bustling with life, but as it turned out, Levi slept through the entire service and didn't make a peep. Charli had tried to pay attention to the homily and what was happening at the altar, but her mind kept wandering back to her problems and she prayed for guidance.

How was she going to convince Martha that she could run the ranch on her own? She knew her mom would never believe her no matter how many times she tried to explain. Her emotions were in turmoil, and part of it was how she felt about her mother.

Even after all these years, she was angry at Martha for leaving her father. Her parents had never shared the reasons for their divorce. It had come as a shock, because John and Martha had kept their arguments behind closed doors. That didn't stop Charli from blaming her mother for the break. And despite Daddy's letter urging her to the contrary, she had no desire whatsoever to reconcile with her sisters.

And then there was Henry, who was now basically a single dad working as a ranch hand with a four-month-old baby to care for and a legal guardianship to pursue. How was all this going to work out in the end?

What a gnarled mess of knots. How would she ever begin to untangle them?

The answer came to her just after midnight on Sunday

evening. She'd been tossing and turning, her brain muddled as she was unable to quiet her thoughts down, when suddenly she sat up straight in bed.

She'd thought of an answer. Way out in left field, maybe, but...

It could work.

Nothing about her idea would be easy. Her first seemingly impassable mountain would be convincing Henry of the rightness of her notion, and it was only going to get steeper from there if they tried to pull it off.

But it *could* work.

She wanted to ride down to Henry's cabin immediately to share her solution, but since it was the middle of the night, she refrained from the urge. What she had to say to Henry would have to wait until morning. She lay back down and curled on her side, her mind still whirling.

There were plans to make. Lots of plans. And the more answers she worked out before morning, the better her pitch to Henry would be.

She finally dropped off to sleep in the early hours from sheer exhaustion, but as was her usual practice as a woman who'd spent her whole life working a ranch, she was up with the dawn. She might have been groggy were it not for the adrenaline racing through her.

This day could very well change everything.

She hurriedly dressed and headed for the stable to tack up Percy for her daily ride to Henry's. She momentarily considered driving down in an ATV, but she needed to do the morning herd check anyway and Percy needed to stretch.

She found Henry outside his cabin chopping wood, the long sleeves of his white Henley pulled up above his elbows, baby Levi sleeping comfortably and safely on the porch in his new bouncer.

Charli couldn't help but admire Henry's strong forearms as he worked. He'd always been in great shape because of the variety of jobs he performed at the ranch, and the ripple of muscles that threaded across his shoulders and arms when he split logs in half with one easy motion was a sight to see.

When he saw her, he landed the axe in the stump he used to prop the logs on and dabbed the sweat on his forehead with the corner of his shirt.

"Hey," he said with a welcoming grin. "I thought I'd get some wood chopped while Levi slept, but now that you're here, do you mind watching him for a few? I'll go out and check the herd."

Charli usually helped him with the task. It was one of many chores they shared. It took two ranchers to do the job well and quickly, but someone had to stay back and watch the baby. That was yet another problem, and they'd soon have to figure out a more permanent solution. But for today, she decided she'd check the herd herself and let Henry stay and bond with his baby.

She'd probably want to get away for a bit after she made her proposition to Henry, anyway. Even thinking about it was making her face warm.

"I'll check the herd. You stay here and give your nephew some cuddles. But before I go, I was wondering if we could…grab a cup of coffee and sit down on the porch?" Her voice sounded tight and high, so she cleared her throat. "I have, er, something I need to talk to you about."

"Sure. Have a seat." He gestured toward one of two

rocking chairs he had on his porch, and Charli thought how sweet it would be to see Henry rocking Levi out here on one of these chairs on a nice spring day. The atmosphere of the ranch was so peaceful and quiet, perfect for an infant.

"Here you go," Henry said as he came out from the kitchen and handed her a hot cup of coffee. He covered a yawn with the back of his hand and sat on the other rocking chair, digging in his heels and leaning back, then taking a sip of the dark brew. "So, what's up?"

Charli blew on her coffee to cool it and then took a large gulp that nearly singed her throat. Now that she was here, face-to-face with Henry, she wondered if her idea really had merit or if she was about to blow her friendship with him to smithereens. As much as she needed things to change and to get a handle on what was happening, she would hate to ruin her relationship with Henry because she'd overstepped the boundaries between them.

"Charli? You okay?" he asked, leaning forward, his forearms on his knees, and cocking his head to meet her gaze. "You looked a little lost there for a moment."

She blew out a breath. "Yeah. Yeah. I'm okay. I have a lot on my mind."

"With everything going on, I'm not surprised."

Levi stirred, and Henry set aside his coffee mug and picked up the baby, pressing him to his shoulder and patting his back. It had only been a few days, and Charli was amazed at how natural Henry looked with Levi.

"I just…don't quite know how to ask you this," she said, forcing herself to press on.

"You know you can ask me anything," he said, his warm voice a gentle rumble.

"Yes. Of course. I know that." She paused. "We're friends, right?"

His eyebrows rose. "Is that how you think of me? As a friend?"

"We've never talked about it, but you know I'd do anything for you."

"As I would for you. I've got your back. But I...work for you," he reminded her, his voice dropping. "At the end of the day, I'm your employee, and you're my boss."

"What if we changed that?" she asked tentatively.

He frowned, his face losing all color. "Are you firing me? Is it because of Levi? Because—"

"What?" she interrupted, cutting him off before he could finish his thought. "No! I don't want to sack you."

He looked relieved. "That's good to hear. What, then?"

"I want to marry you."

Wow. That had come out *way* blunter than she'd intended, so it was no surprise when Henry looked as if someone had punched him in the gut. His gaze widened and his jaw literally dropped.

"Back up a second here." He held one hand in the air, palm out. "Roll it back. I'm not sure I understand."

"You want to stay on the Stafford ranch, don't you?" she asked, sitting taller in her chair and holding her breath. Her mom's suggestion that he might want to leave, especially now that he had Levi to think about, had crossed her mind more than once, haunting her with the possibility.

To her relief, he immediately nodded and took a long sip from his mug. "This ranch is home to me."

"It is to me, as well. And as you know, Martha is trying to push me to sell, meaning you may lose your job if the new owners have their own ranch hands. My mom thinks I can't do it on my own. And frankly, she's probably right. Yes, I've been here all my life, but running a ranch isn't a one-person job."

"I said this earlier, and I'll say it again. I'm here to help you."

"Yes, you are. But when I pointed that out, Martha reminded me that you could decide to leave at any time. And that's true, especially now that you have Levi to think about. I don't have any hold over you."

"So...let me get this right. You want to marry me to hogtie me to the ranch and prove something to your mom?"

Ouch. Granted, her proposal was way out there, but he didn't have to put it quite that way. Charli's guard immediately went up.

"Come on, Henry. That's not what I mean. If we were married, we could hold on to the ranch together. At least think about it. This would be a business arrangement, and I think we can be successful at it. We can have a long engagement if that's what you need, so we'll both know we can make it work before we commit to anything permanent. And this isn't just for me and my problems with the ranch. Consider how much easier it will be for you to obtain guardianship over Levi if the court sees that you have a wife by your side, that Levi will be part of a family unit. We'll be partners in everything, and that piece of paper between us will benefit us both. Please. Just think about it."

He would benefit from having a *wife* by his side. That's what she'd said.

A *wife*.

What was he even supposed to do with that? His head was reeling.

Talk about out of the blue.

Levi was slurping out of his bottle as Henry rocked him. Charli had taken off to check on the cattle the moment after she'd laid out her proposal—because that's what it was, wasn't it? Or as she'd called it, a *business arrangement*.

He had to admit her idea had merit. If he had a wife, getting a judge to grant him guardianship of Levi would be a whole lot less complicated—being able to offer the baby a mom and dad, a nuclear family, instead of just a single father. And courts and judges aside, wouldn't Levi benefit from having a mother?

On the other hand, he knew Charli would be there for Levi either way, whether they did something as outrageous as get married or not. As for Charli keeping the ranch, hadn't he already told her he'd do anything for her? She didn't have to make such a permanent commitment for him to support her.

If he dug deep into his heart and got completely honest with himself, the real problem with marrying Charli wasn't that she'd thought of it first or the ways it would help them both.

It was the way she'd presented a potential union as a *business arrangement*. This wasn't about feelings. Charli hadn't displayed the least bit of emotion, neither happy nor distressed, when she'd proposed marriage as the answer to all their problems.

But what had he expected? If she'd come to him claiming she was in love with him, he wouldn't have believed that for a moment.

He knew perfectly well *those* feelings only went one way, like a rushing river headed toward the ocean. Henry cared for Charli, more than he should. He always had.

But though he acknowledged it inwardly, he would never have acted on those wayward emotions. He wouldn't ever have asked her out on a date, much less tried to pursue a relationship with her.

Now she was offering him the chance to achieve his goal of a permanent partnership in the ranch he loved, but not the relationship he'd long dreamed of. That was a huge step up for him. Otherwise, he didn't know when or if he'd ever have a ranch of his own. And that was not to mention having someone by his side to help him raise Levi.

Yet he felt oddly offended.

He'd asked for time to think about it, and she hadn't pressed him or put a deadline on him making a decision, but a heavy weight built in his chest, and he knew he wouldn't be able to live with the indecision for long without going bonkers.

If it weren't for Levi and for Charli's predicaments, he knew exactly how he'd answer her proposal—with a resounding *no way*. How could his heart handle being with her every day, not just working with her, but living with her, when she looked at him only as—*what*? A ranch hand? An answer to her problems? Or, the best he could hope for, being slotted clearly in the friend zone? But the whole reason she'd made the proposal was for those exact issues, things that needed to be addressed right away. Could he really deny Charli in her hour of need, in helping her keep her ranch or ignoring what was best for Levi?

He needed to think logically here. If he did this, if he said yes to her, he would totally commit to being a good husband. For him, he intended to get married once and for the rest of his life. He'd always longed for a family, although he hadn't ever thought it might happen the way this was turning out, like a runaway freight train. He liked

Charli and knew her character. She would be a wonderful, considerate wife, although she might never reciprocate his feelings. Which meant he would need to keep the fact that he liked her—much more than he should—to himself.

If he could wrangle his emotions, maybe this could work out.

"What do you think, Levi? Do you want a new mama?" he asked the baby as he shifted him to his shoulder and patted him lightly on the back, nuzzling his black tuft of hair with the scruff on his chin. It was amazing how quickly he was adapting to this whole fatherhood thing. In a matter of days, he was already used to feeding and changing little Levi and hardly had to think about what he was doing anymore.

"So, what's the little guy's answer?" Charli asked, leaning against the deck rail.

Henry's adrenaline jolted. He hadn't heard Charli approach from around the side of the cabin. She'd already dismounted and had apparently left Percy to graze in the grass.

Henry caught Charli's gaze and held it for a long moment. There was no doubt in her eyes, nor was there any other emotion. He swallowed hard, his Adam's apple bobbing almost painfully.

Could he really do this?

He'd made his decision, but it was still hard to say it out loud. "Okay."

Her beautiful blue eyes widened, almost as if she was surprised by his answer.

Had she thought he was going to refuse her? Was this some kind of a test?

He mentally backpedaled, but her expression relaxed.

"Okay?" she repeated. "Okay, you'll marry me?"

He nodded. "Yes. Let's get hitched. I agree this is the best thing for Levi. And for you and the ranch."

"Wait." Her face took on a pained expression. "Don't you see how you benefit from this arrangement?"

"This isn't really about me, but I've thought it through, and I'm good with it."

"The ranch," she reminded him. "You'll be on the deed of the ranch."

Henry would be here working the ranch with or without a signature on a deed, but he had to admit the thought of owning something excited him.

He tried to give her his best smile, though he thought it fell short. "Let's do this."

"Okay, then," she said, though she still didn't look completely certain. Was she second-guessing her own idea?

Levi was sleeping, his thumb in his mouth, so Henry gestured for Charli to follow him inside. He placed Levi in his crib and adjusted the baby monitor, then led Charli to the living room.

"When do you want to tie the knot?" he asked.

"We have time to figure that out. I do want to tell my mom right away, though, so she can stop with all her nonsense machinations against me already. I'm going to go find her now. Want to come with? I'd like you to be there when she hears the news about the two of us, and I'd especially like to introduce her to my future son. She's suddenly going to be a grandmother. Surprise! Can you imagine?"

His heart raced at her words. It was a lot. He wondered once again if he'd just made the biggest mistake of his life.

Chapter Four

She waited for tears to come—tears of anger, not grief. Bitterness and frustration. But even that release had been denied to her. Her tear ducts seemed to have dried up completely. And just when she'd thought she'd come up with a reasonable solution to all her problems, her mother had nixed the whole plan. Had practically laughed at the thought of Charli wedding a ranch hand.

Charli had a hard time seeing her mother's point of view. Once upon a time, Martha had fallen in love with and married a ranch hand. Was that what this was really all about? Was she comparing Charli's situation to her own past, her own complicated feelings about living on a ranch and the painful emotions of ending her relationship with Daddy?

That was hardly fair, comparing her situation to Charli's, but then again, none of what Charli had recently experienced was, starting with her father's excruciating scheme.

Would this nightmare ever end?

She'd been so positive presenting Henry as her fiancé would have made a difference to her mother, proof that Henry was going to stay. A husband-to-be and a future son should have squared things away as far as the ranch was concerned, but if anything, Martha had stiffened her upper lip and doubled down on the idea of Charli selling the ranch and making a *real life* for herself.

As if ranching wasn't a real life. How many times could they argue about that? But Charli supposed she couldn't blame her mom for feeling a little ganged up on, especially since she'd confronted her straight out with the news of her engagement without buffering it in any way. Her mother had said she was only thinking about what would be best for Charli, and though it was hard for Charli to accept, her mother had her right to her opinions—as long as they didn't become facts.

Maybe her mother hadn't enjoyed her life on the ranch with Charli's father and had escaped as soon as she could. Martha had grown up in the country, but that didn't necessarily mean that type of living was right for her the way it was for Charli. For all Charli knew, perhaps disliking country living was part of the reason Martha had divorced John and taken off to Denver with her little sisters. But whatever Martha's opinions and feelings about where she'd been raised and spent the first few years of her married life, Charli had found great joy working the ranch, and she couldn't imagine living anywhere else.

She would fight this battle, and she would continue fighting until she won.

Heat and furious adrenaline had coursed through her. Why was grief so hard to absorb when anger so easily flared?

As if the back and forth butting heads with her mother wasn't enough, Martha had absolutely refused to acknowledge their engagement, much less embrace the idea of Charli adopting Levi as her son. While her mom's expression had softened for a moment as Henry showed her his nephew, she'd quickly turned back to her point, which was that Charli would be making the biggest mistake of her life if she "handed the ranch over to Henry," even if that were possible, which it was not, at least until they'd settled her father's last wishes between them. And even then, she and Henry would be equal partners in everything. He wasn't stealing anything away from her.

Martha had spoken as though Henry wasn't in the room, hat in hand, listening to every word. Charli had flashed him an apologetic gaze, but he hadn't stepped forward and defended himself. His dark brows had lowered over those intelligent, striking blue eyes, but other than that he hadn't reacted.

Charli had known she was hitting Martha right between the eyes with a huge surprise coming out of nowhere, and that may have been unfair, but that didn't make it wrong. As it was, she herself was still coming to terms with the idea of getting married. It felt surreal. She would never have considered it were it not for the extenuating circumstances.

Martha had tried to put her foot down, but Charli would have none of it. She'd argued that it wasn't as if she was handing Henry the deed to the ranch outright. She and Henry would be partners in work and in life. In her mind, working the land together was at least as good of a reason to tie the knot as love and romance, which in her limited experience faded with time and often turned into something ugly. She had to look no further than her mother and father. They'd ended up miserable together and both had been much happier after they'd split up.

Emotions? No, thank you. She'd stick with logic.

If—*when*—she and Henry married, she'd willingly

commit to living the rest of her life with him and would try to be the best wife and mother she could be. She was determined to ride on this particular merry-go-round only once in her life. Though marriage had been the furthest thing from her mind just a couple of weeks ago, the thought didn't bother her as much as perhaps it ought to have.

She'd felt at peace about her decision until she and Henry, Levi in tow, had left her mother and returned to his small cabin to put the baby down for a nap. Then, after Henry not saying a single word while she'd been painfully laying out their plans to Martha, all of a sudden it appeared he had a lot to say.

He laid a sleeping Levi in his crib and then returned to face her, scratching his dark, scruffy cheek as he so often did when he was deep in thought. He shifted from boot to boot and cleared his throat before speaking.

"Your mother is right, you know," he started, his voice tight and even, his face without expression.

It had already been an especially tough day for her without Henry hopping on the *you can't do it* bandwagon. She'd thought he believed in her. She certainly wouldn't have asked him to partner up with her if he didn't. She immediately tensed, feeling as ruffled as a cat whose fur was being petted from tail to head, her hackles up as she hissed her next words.

"What's that supposed to mean?" she demanded.

"Exactly what your mom said. I'm not good enough for you."

She was so surprised, both by what he was saying and how miserable he sounded saying it, that she gaped, but he stuffed his hands into the front pockets of his jeans and turned his gaze away from her, suddenly interested in something on the floor.

Oh, no. This was *not* going to happen. He was *so* not going to bail on her right after they'd—well, *she'd*—confronted her mother and made their engagement into a reality.

"Don't say that. Don't even *think* it," she said, her voice turning ragged. "We've already made this decision and made a big deal of it to Martha. You can't turn your back on me now. I wouldn't have chosen you as my partner if I didn't genuinely think this could work out between us. Remember, we're doing this for Levi. You can't let that little boy down."

She knew she was piling on the guilt, but she was feeling more than a little bit desperate, and Henry had never let her down before.

"And my—our...*our*—ranch," she added, stuttering through her words. It was a totally different way of thinking for her, the Stafford ranch belonging to anyone but Staffords, but it would be true soon enough. She may as well accept this new normal and get used to it.

He sighed and scrubbed a hand through his hair. "We're so different, and I'm not even sure you can see it. You're so wildly intelligent, and I'm...not that smart," he countered.

That's when the anger started in earnest. She wasn't upset with anyone in particular. Not Henry. Not even Martha. Just with this whole blooming mess. How had she managed to dig herself into this—and how was she ever going to get out?

"I don't believe that," she said, trying to soften her tone when inside she felt like screaming in frustration. "I admire you so much. Why else would I have asked you to marry me? So what about book learning? There are many ways to show your intelligence. You know everything there is to know about working the Stafford ranch, and there is no one I trust more with my cattle and the land."

And with me, she added silently. Henry was the only man she could trust to be her true partner in life.

"Your mom is never going to accept me as your equal. She doesn't believe my GED is worth anything because I dropped out of school at sixteen. That makes me a quitter in her eyes, and maybe she's right. I did bail when things got tough. I can't go back and change things even if I wanted to."

"You heard Mom and me talking that first day?" Charli queried, angry with her mother all over again for voicing her opinions about Henry aloud.

"I was still in the mudroom putting on my boots. I wasn't trying to eavesdrop, and Martha wasn't exactly whispering. I couldn't help but overhear, especially after I heard you say my name. Thank you for sticking up for me, by the way."

"There's a big difference between book smart and ranch smart," she reminded him again, catching and holding his charged gaze. "Yes, I got my college degree to help my dad on the ranch, but honestly, I could have easily lived this life without it. You don't need academic letters behind your name to be a successful rancher. You're excellent at what you do without having gone to university. And more than that, you're a good person. At the end of the day, that's what really counts. Your character."

"Hmm." He clearly didn't believe her.

"I wish you wouldn't view your neurodiversity as making you inferior in some way. I know being different from the status quo can be a challenge sometimes, but that's how God made you. Accept it and embrace it. You're unique in a *good* way. And you've got a genuine heart, which is a lot more than I can say about most people I know. I asked you to marry me for a reason, Henry. Together, I know we can make this ranch a success and be good guardians to Levi. We just need to keep our focus on what's important. Keep our eyes on the prize."

"I guess."

"You don't believe me," Charli stated. It wasn't a question. She pressed her palm to his jaw, her thumb brushing across his cheek.

He shrugged. She wanted to take him by those broad, muscular shoulders and shake him until he listened and accepted the truth, but she supposed it would take more than one conversation for him to adjust the way he'd thought of himself for the whole thirty-six years he'd been living with his challenges.

She would be his friend through thick and thin, just as she always had been. Yes, their relationship was bound to change once they were married, but if anything, that would make it easier for her to support him until eventually he could see himself through her eyes.

As a man worth holding on to.

Henry's head was spinning. He didn't know what to think, much less what to say to Charli. Was that really how she saw him? And if it was, how could he ever live up to her expectations?

He vowed to start now, showing Charli he could be a man whose shoulder she could lean on when the going got tough. That was why she'd asked him to marry her in the first place, and right now he knew she was carrying a tremendous burden. It was a lot.

For *them* to carry.

The two shall become one.

He swallowed hard as his gut turned over. He was experiencing all the feels—happiness, giddiness, an enormous sense of responsibility and yes, feeling overwhelmed. How could he not? But he reminded himself for the thousandth time in the past week that Charli didn't feel the same way about him as he did about her. She was stressed and besieged and had seen marrying him as her way out. He wouldn't add to her anxiety by burdening her with his own problems, his unreciprocated emotions.

When he'd accidentally and without conscious thought mentioned backing out, she'd had a clear moment of panic. He'd been able to read it in her expression, and he didn't want to do that to her again. He still felt he wasn't good enough for her, but since this marriage was what she wanted, he was determined he would step up and really commit his heart, mind and body to it.

While he could tell her what he was thinking, he'd much rather show her, to reassure her he'd meant what he said. But what could he do to display his support for their engagement in a way that would mean something to Charli?

The answer came to him immediately. If things were different, if he'd been the one to propose, he would have presented her with an engagement ring down on one knee. But their engagement hadn't been in any way conventional. She deserved a grand gesture and a huge rock on her finger, though he suspected she wasn't the type of woman who'd want a giant diamond. It wasn't her style. But even if it was, he'd just spent a bundle on baby stuff and didn't really have that much in the bank, and what he did have he needed to save for his new family.

Another idea suddenly crossed his mind in a flash. Why hadn't he thought of it before?

"I'll be right back," he told Charli, then headed for his spare bedroom closet, which he used as extra storage space in the small cabin. He tiptoed in, as the room itself was now Levi's nursery, and the baby was sound asleep in his crib.

Quietly so as not to wake Levi, he reached up to the topmost closet shelf and took down a very old shoebox, one in which his mom used to keep what she called his "treasures." The shoebox was decorated with ribbons, but he could still see the picture on the top of the box, which was of the specially crafted black-and-white leather shoes he'd worn as a small child to correct his pigeon toes.

He missed his mother and father and wished things were different between them, but now wasn't the time to stroll down memory lane. He was after something specific. He lifted the lid and sorted through the items, which were mostly old pictures of him as a boy. There was no schoolwork, as Henry had never gotten good grades worthy of keeping. No artwork, either, because Henry hadn't been artistic in any way. What he'd always been good at—caring for animals—couldn't fit into a shoebox.

It took him a minute, but he finally found what he was looking for—his grandmother's antique diamond and sapphire ring. She'd given it to him before she'd passed, explaining that his grandfather had given it to her on their wedding day, and she hoped Henry would give it to the woman he married. He didn't know why it had skipped generations, or she'd chosen him instead of Jamie Lynn. Maybe it was because Gran and Henry had always had an especially close relationship. But he was glad he'd remembered it now. Charli may not be the type to want an enormous diamond engagement ring, but she *was* the type of woman who would appreciate an antique ring passed down through generations.

He pocketed the ring and was heading back to the living room, considering the best way to present it to her without looking like a dork, when he heard Charli talking to someone. He paused in the hallway, trying to identify the voice. It only took him a moment to realize the excited whisper belonged to Charli's middle sister, Fiona.

"Mama said you guys have a baby here," Fiona said as Henry entered the room, and she greeted him with a friendly wave. "Hi, Henry!"

He nodded his head at her.

"Levi is Henry's nephew," Charli affirmed with a nod. "Due to a series of circumstances with his sister, we're planning to apply for permanent guardianship of the little guy."

"We?" Fiona's eyes widened in surprise.

"Yes. Henry and I."

"How exciting. But... I—I don't understand," Fiona stammered, crinkling her brows over her nose. "Why—or rather, *how* are you both applying for guardianship? I feel as if there's something major I missed."

Fiona paused, for once speechless, and Henry stepped forward and took Charli's hand, linking her fingers through his. "We're getting hitched."

Fiona's jaw dropped. "I didn't even realize you two

were in a relationship, and I definitely didn't know you were getting married. Charli…how did I not hear about this? It seems like a pretty big oversight not to tell your family about your engagement, if you ask me."

Charli stiffened and stepped closer to Henry. "It's very recent. We only just decided to get married."

He squeezed her hand. There hadn't been any communication between Charli and her sisters in twenty years, so in his opinion there was no reason to assume she would let Fiona know anything about her personal life, now or in the past. But he wasn't going to speak his thoughts aloud, especially since Charli didn't seem to be in a hurry to correct her sister. Fiona didn't need to know he and Charli hadn't ever been dating.

"How exciting," Fiona said. "Congratulations to both of you on your engagement, and on adopting your new baby." She sounded genuine enough, and Henry found himself liking her more than he'd expected to, though Charli was still standing stiffly beside him, her hand clenched in his. Clearly, nothing about this moment was easy for her.

At that moment, the baby wailed for attention.

Fiona's grin widened. "I was hoping he'd wake up while I was here. May I see him?" she asked, her enthusiasm bursting through every pore. Henry wondered how the vivacious Fiona could even be related to over-serious, overthinking Charli. They were worlds apart in looks and personality. Fiona probably rubbed Charli like sandpaper, if he didn't miss his guess.

"Sure," Henry said, stepping in and answering for Charli. He figured at the end of the day Levi was his nephew, and thus his responsibility to introduce to those who would eventually be his extended family. "Hold on a sec and I'll go get him."

He was surprised how proud he felt as he scooped Levi into his arms, tucking the baby onto his shoulder as he brought him into the living room to introduce him to Fiona. His chest welled with gratification for the baby.

What astonished him even more than his own feelings was how delighted Charli appeared as she took the baby into her arms and then handed him to Fiona.

"This is baby Levi," Charli said, brushing a hand over the baby's soft curls. "Isn't he precious?"

"And you said he's your nephew?" Fiona prodded, glancing at Henry and making him suddenly feel as if red ants were crawling all over his skin. He would *so* rather be out in the field on his horse, watching over the cattle in his care. Her curiosity was discernibly palpable, as were his snapping nerves.

"Levi is Henry's sister's child," Charli said, jumping into the fray and sending Henry an apologetic glance. "We'd prefer not to share any legal details about what's happening until we've wrapped up the court case."

"Of course. I completely understand," Fiona said softly, not appearing at all taken aback or offended by the way Charli had brought the conversation to a firm close. "He is a real sweetheart. Look at these chubby cheeks. I'll bet you both love him already."

Henry swallowed hard. He honestly didn't know how he felt and couldn't put it into words. He knew he felt *something*. Levi and Charli were more to him than just a duty, a problem for him to handle. There were definitely serious emotions involved with both Charli and Levi. But he was a long way from processing every thought charging through his head and every feeling galloping through his heart.

"I didn't mean to disturb you. I'll let you two get on with your day," Fiona said, giving Levi one last kiss on the top of his head before handing him back to Henry, who held him outward, curved in one arm. "I'm sure you have a lot to do between the baby and the ranch."

"I'll say," Charli murmured in agreement.

"If you need anything, feel free to call on me." Fiona's expression brightened. "You know what? I think I can help."

Charli lifted one blond eyebrow. "How is that, exactly?" She sounded suspicious, as well she might. The sisters were just getting to know one another, and the circumstances of their past were hardly suggestive of being able to form a close relationship, especially this quickly. Fiona didn't appear to recognize that.

"With the baby, I mean. I know you and Henry have a lot of work to do on the ranch every day. I'm going to be here for a while, I think, at least until we work out all the details of our father's estate. I love children. I could babysit for you if you want. I worked as a nanny for a couple of years just out of high school. I used that time to make money for college. I'd love to watch Levi for you while I'm here."

Charli didn't look convinced, but as far as Henry was concerned, Fiona may very well be an answer to prayer. He genuinely liked her. She appeared trustworthy, and she was Charli's sister, after all, even if they hadn't seen each other in forever.

He captured Charli's gaze and silently asked her opinion. He would defer to her either way in this, despite his own feelings. He didn't want to put her in an uncomfortable position.

"Are you sure it won't be a problem?" Charli asked at last.

"Absolutely not."

"We keep ranch hours. Sunup until sundown. Although on the days we need you, one or the other of us, sometimes both of us, will be back to care for Levi from time to time throughout the day," Charli said, looking to Henry for validation.

"I'm a morning person. Call me anytime you need me."

Fiona was gone as quickly as she had arrived, flitting away like the butterfly she reminded Henry of.

Charli turned to Henry, who was allowing the hungry baby to gum his pointer finger. "Well, that was interesting," she said.

"I like her," Henry admitted, gesturing for Charli to follow him into the kitchen so he could measure formula powder into a bottle and add warmed distilled water. He passed Levi to her so he could make up a bottle.

Charli sighed wearily. "I have to confess I think I like her, too. She isn't at all what I was expecting." She bounced lightly on her toes to keep Levi comfortable.

"Maybe we should keep our minds open where the others are concerned, as well?" Henry spoke softly and framed the sentence as a question. He knew Charli still carried a lot of bitterness in her heart, and no wonder.

"Well, I have to admit having the choice of Fiona watching Levi will solve a big problem, at least in the short-term." Charli brushed the back of her fingers across her high cheekbone and Henry followed the movement with his eyes.

She was so striking she took his breath away. She always had.

And now she would be his to love and protect.

He swallowed hard, forcing his feelings to subside, pressing his emotions deep into his gut as he shoved his hands into the front pockets of his jeans, where one fist closed around *the ring*.

After Fiona had arrived so unexpectedly, he'd nearly forgotten he was going to give it to her.

He hadn't even thought about the best way to do it without looking like a total goof.

Clearing his throat, he dropped to one knee before he could think better of it.

Chapter Five

"What do you think?" Charli asked, still feeling off-kilter from her sister's surprise visit. "Should we give Fiona the job? On one hand, it would be an answer to prayer not to have to scramble to look for someone else on the spur of the moment. On the other hand, even though we're related, I don't know her well enough to know for sure we can trust her with the baby."

She turned to face Henry, only to find he wasn't there.

Well, he was *there*, but he wasn't standing right behind her as she'd expected. He'd dropped to one knee and was looking up at her, his expression serious as he held out a *ring* between his thumb and forefinger. He was looking decidedly uncomfortable as he gazed up at her, his face flushed to a cherry red and his shoulders as stiff as a board. His jaw worked, but no words emerged from his lips.

"Henry," Charli squeaked, pressing a hand to her heart. "What are you doing down there? Get up this instant!"

"I—I—just thought you…that is, I want to give you this ring, Charli," he stammered. "I figured…in order to make our engagement official…you ought to have a ring. So you can show everyone we're serious about this." He stopped and cleared his throat again, then continued.

"Charlotte Marie Stafford, will you be my wife?" His tone was stiff, formal and completely in earnest.

Her full name sounded amazing rumbling through his full, rich voice from deep in his throat, and Charli's pulse roared to life. A shiver of gooseflesh ran through her despite her surprise and confusion. She hadn't been remotely ready for him to turn this proposal around on her, and she definitely hadn't been prepared to experience such a visceral response to his words. She'd never been a romantic, nor the type of woman who'd ever dreamed of the perfect way a man would propose to her, dropping down onto one knee, no less, just like in the movies. Daydreams of her wedding day, of picking out a dress and flowers, of what married life would be like and starting a family... those things hadn't even been on her radar and had, in fact, been the furthest thing from her mind, at least until Martha had pressed her to do something truly desperate by threatening to snatch her ranch away from her. Then Levi had suddenly and unexpectedly entered Henry's life and had made the necessity of getting married a double whammy of her life.

Their lives.

This was Henry.

Henry. The man she considered her best friend.

The thought was at the same time both soothing and stunning.

"There's no need for you to do this," she protested. "You know me better than anyone. I don't need grand gestures to show we mean it. We've already agreed that we're going to tie the knot, and that's good enough for me. Please. Just stand up. You're embarrassing me." She reached for his hands, pulling him to his feet.

She was experiencing a swirl of emotions that went far beyond just being uncomfortable, but she refused to examine anything she was currently feeling too closely for fear it would ruin everything they'd worked so hard to plan. She hoped Henry realized how vital it was to keep this arrangement on a strictly platonic business level. Other kinds of emotions would complicate an already complicated situation, and they couldn't afford that right now.

"Look," he said, holding the palm of his hand out to her. "Please. Just look at it."

Inside his hand was the most beautiful ring she'd ever seen, a small but glistening diamond solitaire surrounded by half-moon sapphires that were the exact color of Henry's eyes.

It was perfect in every way and completely reminded her of Henry. She hadn't really ever imagined receiving an engagement ring of any kind, but if she had, this would have been it.

Again she experienced an odd fluttering in her stomach.

"This is beautiful," she admitted, "but you didn't need to buy me a ring. This must have cost you a fortune."

She didn't understand Henry at all. With everything that they were now up against, why was he spending money she knew he didn't have on a ring she didn't need?

"I...didn't buy it," he told her, his voice rough with emotion. "This is my grandmother's ring, an antique my grandfather gave her on their wedding day. She wanted me to give it to my wife, and since that's going to be you, I figured you should have it. And—and I thought I should propose," he stammered.

Charli didn't like where this was going, and panic rose in her chest, embers burning through her. She felt as if she were on a runaway train about to go off a cliff, the wheels sparking as the brakes attempted to keep her from falling. There was no room for sentiment in their relationship, she reminded herself, despite all the erratic feelings she was currently experiencing. She couldn't handle one more thing in her life, up to and including even the suggestion of a romantic relationship.

But she didn't want to hurt his feelings, either. While she didn't exactly understand his reasoning, he'd obviously put a lot of thought into this, and his grandmother's ring clearly meant something special to him. She didn't know how to let him down easily.

"Henry?"

"Charli?" he echoed in the exact same tone she'd just used.

She couldn't help but chuckle. That was one thing about Henry. He'd always been able to lighten the mood, even when she was being ridiculously serious as she knew she was being right now.

"So, do you want to wear this thing or not?" His question was stated so casually that if she didn't know him as well as she did, she'd think it didn't matter to him one way or the other. But she could see in his gaze that it did.

"Oh, Henry. Of course I'll wear your ring," she said, shifting Levi to her right shoulder and holding out her left hand. His hand quivered as he placed the ring on her finger. "But—you know this doesn't change anything, right? This—" she gestured between the two of them "—is still a business arrangement at the end of the day.

We're committed to doing what's best for the ranch and for Levi. Right?"

He paused for a moment, his gaze narrowing, but finally he echoed her words. "Right. A business arrangement."

She couldn't help but admire the sparkle on her left hand. It shimmered every time she moved.

It makes sense, she told herself, to wear a ring to show Martha and her sisters they were serious about getting married. It would be a constant reminder to everyone, including herself, that she and Henry were going to make this work.

"I admit this is a good idea. But no more surprises, okay?" she said, trying to keep her tone light and playful so as not to hurt Henry's feelings. "I think we've had enough of those to last a lifetime."

Henry nodded in agreement. "It's not every day a baby lands on your doorstep, or in this case, in my kitchen, with a note that says he's now mine to care for and love."

"Levi's not just any baby." She cooed nonsense words to the child. "You're a precious blessing, aren't you, little guy?"

She glanced at Henry, but he wasn't smiling. A flash of pain lit his gaze before he shuttered his thoughts. She wondered what he was thinking but couldn't begin to guess.

"So, then, we understand one another?" she asked, transferring the baby to his arms and reaching for his hand.

He swallowed and nodded, his gaze giving away nothing.

"Good. Come by my office later today and we can start

filling out the paperwork for Levi's guardianship. That seems to be the first order of business, don't you think?"

"Will do," he said, his voice gravelly. He cleared his throat.

"Good," she said again, then smiled and impulsively leaned up on tiptoe to plant a gentle, friendly kiss on his scruffy cheek. "I'll see you then."

Henry stood silently for a long time after Charli had left, his palm pressed to his cheek as if sealing the spot where her soft lips had met his rough skin. On paper, he knew exactly what he was getting into, but the more time he spent with Charli, the foggier the situation became in his mind and heart. Did she not even realize she was sending him mixed signals?

Or was he simply overthinking everything? It wouldn't be the first time. Maybe he was the one sending her mixed signals, with the ring and all. It had seemed like a good idea at the time, but now he wondered if he'd made the wrong choice, given how reluctantly she'd accepted it.

For the millionth time since he'd first agreed to this arrangement, he wondered if it was the best thing for them both. Well, for him, anyway. Running the ranch together and having a permanent partner who had his back with Levi notwithstanding, how was he supposed to turn his heart off? It wasn't as if he could flip off an emotional switch.

For the first time since they'd agreed to wed, it occurred to him that he hadn't thought past the wedding day. Their engagement, which almost felt counterfeit in many ways, had been in his mind nonstop since the moment he'd agreed to it, but what about after they exchanged vows? Were they to have a counterfeit marriage, as well?

The best thing to do where Charli was concerned was to ask her outright what her intentions were after they were wed. She was a straight shooter and would tell him the truth. It was one of the reasons he so admired her. If they were going to fake a relationship their whole lives, it was better for him to know now.

If she didn't intend to marry him for real, he wasn't sure he could go through with it. Yes, he had Levi now, but he also wanted children of his own. And yes, he was getting a ranch in this exchange, but he wanted little ones to grow up here and love the country just as much as he did.

He bundled Levi into his car seat and drove up to the main ranch house where Charli had her office. It had a side entrance coming in from outside, so thankfully, he didn't have to run the risk of encountering Martha or either of Charli's sisters.

When he entered the office, he found Charli hunching over a number of spreadsheets she'd printed out, her fingers busily tapping on an adding machine that was spewing out rows of numbers in a thin paper line, the *punch, punch, cha-ching* a familiar sound.

"Whatcha doing?" he asked, sitting down opposite her and spreading out his legs, crossing them at the ankles. He hadn't taken Levi out of his car seat because the baby had fallen asleep, so he quietly rocked the car seat with the toe of one boot. Even though Charli was his boss, he was comfortable in her presence—or at least he had been before they'd become engaged. The last thing he wanted was for things to become awkward between them, which was precisely why he had to ask the question hovering on his lips.

Charli looked up and sighed, then brushed her palms back over her head to smooth out her ponytail. "Just crunching numbers. The lawyer is supposed to visit us on Friday to read the will. Since I already know more or less what Daddy has done with it, I'm trying to come up with an alternative we can all live with. I want to have a presentation ready that will make sense to everyone."

"Like what?" Henry asked curiously, glancing down at the baby when he cooed in his sleep. Levi's pursed lips moved as if he were sucking on his bottle, but he didn't wake up. Henry's heart swelled, and he couldn't help but grin at the cute little sleeping tyke.

"I've done some research into Daddy's assets and have discovered he was quite wealthy in his own right, though he never shared that information with me. And I don't know how much Martha is aware of everything he saved. He did well with his investments and left them to my sisters and me in a trust. And here I thought his only focus had been the ranch. As it turns out, he left quite a bit more than just the land—enough for me to split what I would have received as part of the investments between my two sisters and instead keep the ranch for us. I'm hoping I can make a good case for this and all of it can be wrapped up in our favor."

"It sounds like you've done the work. I can't see why they would balk at that setup." Henry scratched the scruff on his chin.

"That's what I'm trying to figure out. I need to know exact figures for the difference between what they would immediately receive in investments and what they would make if we sold the ranch. The problem is if we split the investments three ways and sold the ranch to split among us, it may be more than if they get half the investments alone."

That didn't sound good. "What if that turns out to be the case?"

"Then I'll have to hope they'll see my heart and give me grace. But at the end of the day, we're talking money, and my sisters don't know me from Adam. There's no reason for them to give me any kind of break just because I'm their biological sister. And I don't know how to show them just how much this ranch means to me."

"Maybe if you get Martha on board?" Henry suggested.

"Maybe." Charli looked thoughtful.

"Speaking of your mom," Henry continued, "what about her stake in your father's claim?"

"He set up a trust for her years ago. She apparently refused alimony and wanted to make a clean cut on her own, but Daddy set aside part of his earnings every calving season and placed it in a trust for her. To my knowledge, she's never touched it, but she now knows it's there and she can use it when and if she needs to."

"I can tell you and your sisters come from a long line of strong women. I remember your grandmother back in the day. She was as tough as they came."

He winced inwardly, instantly wishing he could take back the words. Charli's grandmother had passed before John and Martha had divorced, so he was possibly bringing up bad memories for her. He watched her face carefully for a reaction, but her expression was set in stone.

"I'd rather you not compare me to my mother and sisters," she eventually murmured, leaning her elbows on the table and pressing her palms to her tired eyes.

"Sorry. I didn't mean to bring up any painful memories for you."

"No, don't be. I know what you meant to say. And I appreciate the compliment. I very much want to be like my grandma. She was an amazing woman. If I can just work through this, things will be better on the other side. I hope."

"It seems to me you already have a teammate in Fiona."

"The jury is still out on that one. But yes, I am optimistic I can turn her around to my way of thinking. At least she appears open to it."

"Maybe if you try and discover your sisters' future plans, you can approach them that way. Appeal to their higher natures."

"That could be a problem. Cordelia at least hates me. I'm not even sure she'll speak to me."

Henry made a sound low in his throat. "She doesn't know you well enough to hate you."

"Be that as it may, I always feel like she's firing darts at me through her gaze whenever I'm around her."

"Give her a chance. Maybe it's not as bad as all that."

"Humph." Charli shook her head. "If you say so."

"Don't doubt yourself now. You and I need to present a united front where the ranch is concerned. Let them see how much it means to our little family. Don't you think if they see us together, that will help?"

"If I didn't feel that way, I wouldn't have asked you to marry me. What better way to show my mom I'm dedicated to staying here than by tying the knot with you?"

"Exactly." Henry paused a moment before adding,

"And…" He cleared his throat, which had suddenly become rough and scratchy. "Speaking of the ranch?"

"What about it?" The way she asked the question sounded as if she was expecting him to throw something negative at her. And maybe he was, but he needed to know the answer to how he was feeling, and if he shoved the question back down inside without asking it, it would eventually eat him alive.

"I was just thinking about our partnership. I know and agree that this is a business arrangement. I comprehend why you offered it in the first place, and I understand the parameters of our engagement. But what about when it comes to the marriage?"

"What about it?" she asked again, narrowing her gaze in confusion.

"Um…do you, er, want children? Other than Levi, I mean? *Our* children?"

Her gaze then widened to epic proportions, the azure blue of her eyes darkening until just the pupils were showing. "Honestly? I haven't given that much thought to it. Though now that you mention it, it's definitely something I ought to be seriously considering, isn't it?"

Which was exactly what he'd figured she would say. Charli lived in the moment, taking every challenge as it came, and right now she had a ton on her plate.

"That said," she continued thoughtfully, "I intend to be a wife to you in every meaning of the word. So to answer your question, yes, I do want more children in my future. It's just more than I can consider right now. It's too much to think about becoming a mother to future children when I'm still just getting used to thinking about being your wife and a mother to Levi."

He reached across the desk and took her hand, squeezing it lightly. "I understand. I'm not trying to put any pressure on you. Likewise, I want you to know that I'm prepared to be your husband in every way. I will gladly protect you, take care of you and work beside you every day of my life."

"Thank you," she whispered raggedly, "for always having my back. I know this can't be easy for you."

"Not any harder than it is for you. I've got you, Charli. Always."

"Back at you. Whatever we have to do to offer Levi a safe and love-filled life, we will do. Together."

Despite telling himself he wouldn't let it happen, hope swelled in Henry's chest. Maybe there was a future for them after all.

"Oh, and Charli?"

"Hmm?" Charli appeared to be only half listening, having dropped her gaze back to her spreadsheets and her fingers returning to the adding machine.

"As I was driving up here, I noticed one of the cows looked ready to drop. We should probably keep an eye on her tonight. I moved her up to the front pasture."

Charli glanced up, her interest piqued. Calves were the bread and butter of this operation. They always kept a close eye on mamas and babies to make sure the birth was safe, and the calves were suckling. Sometimes mother cows rejected their calves, and they had to be hand reared and bottle-fed. Hopefully everything would go smoothly with this birth, whenever it happened.

"Okay, will do," she said. "Thanks for letting me know. I'll keep an eye on her. You just worry about taking care of Levi."

"I'll be checking, as well," he insisted.

"You have the baby to worry about. I'll do it."

Henry tensed. He didn't want her talking him out of his job, especially since this was now not only his job, but he would soon be in partnership with Charli in running the ranch.

"Even with Levi in tow, I can do this. Things aren't going to change just because I have a baby to take care of. They can't." He knew he sounded stubborn, and maybe he was being stubborn, but he couldn't let her brush him off this way.

She met and held his gaze. He froze, unmoving, as she looked for who knew what in his eyes. Finally, she shrugged and nodded.

"Maybe I'll see you out there, then. Call me if anything comes up in the meantime."

Henry smiled as he exited the office, feeling as if he'd had some wins today. For once, the world wasn't squashing him down. He figured he'd best be appreciating the feeling while it was here to appreciate. Who knew what the future held?

Chapter Six

Charli's cell phone rang just after she'd dropped into a deep sleep. She'd been tossing and turning again. Henry's name lit up the screen and she rolled up to a sitting position, dangling her legs over the side of her bed before answering.

"Henry?" she asked groggily. "What's wrong?"

"Charli," Henry said, alarm piercing through his tight, shrill voice. "I'm so glad you picked up. I was praying you would."

"Is the calf okay?"

"It's not the calf. I checked the cow a little while ago, and I don't think the calf is going to come tonight."

"What is it, then? You don't sound like your regular self."

"I'm not. I don't know what I did, but somehow I must have messed up. There's something wrong with the baby. I'm completely freaking out right now. I don't know what to do." His sentences were clipped, and his breath was coming out in hurried, panicked gasps.

She could picture him with his phone tucked between his chin and broad shoulder as he rocked Levi in his strong arms.

"Take a deep breath and tell me what's wrong," she murmured, keeping her voice low, even and supportive.

"When I put Levi down in his crib for the night after his feeding, he was fine. At least, I think he was okay. I didn't notice anything wrong with him. After about an hour, he started crying. I went into his nursery to pick him up so I could change him and give him a bottle, but I couldn't get him to stop wailing. It sounded different to me than his usual cry. He was extra distressed, and his face was red from crying. And when I went to change his diaper, I about had a heart attack right then and there. Charli, he has tons of spots all over his little body. Big red welts. I don't know what I did to make this happen or how to help him."

"He has hives?" she questioned.

"I don't know. Maybe. And they are seriously everywhere, even on his palms and the bottoms of his feet. I'm at a total loss. I don't know what to do."

"It sounds as if perhaps he's having an allergic reaction to something. Food or your laundry detergent, or something else he may have touched. It's hard to say. Look, it's probably nothing, but I think you ought to take him to the emergency room just to be sure and have a doctor look him over. Better safe than sorry, and that way you'll know what you're dealing with and if there's anything you can do to help the poor tyke. He sounds miserable, and the doctors may be able to give him medicine or something to help him feel better."

"Okay. You're right, as usual. That's why I called you. I knew you'd be able to help me. I'll go straight to the ER. I just have to hurry up and pack his diaper bag first, and then I'll be on my way."

"It's important that you don't panic. And don't drive like a maniac to get to the hospital. It's only a few miles to get to St. Anthony's Regional. It's not worth it to put yourself or Levi in danger."

He sounded as if he was only half listening as she heard him scuffling around in the background, but she hoped he'd take her words to heart.

"Listen, I'll meet you there, okay? In the ER waiting room." The middle of the night or not, she would do anything she could to support Henry and Levi without giving it a second thought. She may not be able to do anything to make Levi feel better, but at least she could be by Henry's side tonight for encouragement.

"Thank you," he said on an exhale. "I'm heading out now." He cut the call before Charli could say goodbye or offer any more words of reassurance.

Charli quickly changed into jeans and a soft pink Henley and pulled on her cowboy boots. It occurred to her as she was dressing that she ought to stop by the office and grab the file folder of Levi's legal documents Jamie Lynn had left them, which they were using to fill out all the necessary court papers to set up a court date to pursue guardianship. She didn't know if they'd need the baby's birth certificate or anything, but better safe than sorry.

Her tires squealed as she pulled out of her gravel driveway and onto the asphalt of the county road. She'd told Henry not to panic and drive too fast, and now she was doing just that herself. As much as she wanted to put the pedal to the metal, she forced herself to drive the speed limit to the hospital, praying all the way for both Levi's and Henry's well-being, then carefully parked in the emergency room lot and grabbed the file folder from the passenger seat beside her. She figured she was only fifteen minutes behind him at most.

Once she was out of the car, though, she broke into a run. Hives could be nothing, she reminded herself. They could mean anything. Everyone she knew suffered from hives once in a while, though it was admittedly scarier with an infant.

She rushed through the automatic double doors so fast they almost didn't open in time. Wouldn't that just have been something, for her to run headlong into the glass? Thankfully, she had paused just in time to allow the doors to open and then darted between them.

She didn't see Henry in the waiting room, so she approached the front desk, waiting impatiently for the clerk to notice her.

"What are we seeing you for today?" the young woman asked politely.

"Oh, it's not me. I'm looking for my friend Henry Parker. He would have brought in a baby boy with hives within the last half hour."

"Of course. They're in triage now. Follow me."

She found Henry slumped in a chair, holding Levi as the nurse took the baby's vitals. Levi was in a fitful sleep and looked as if he'd been crying for some time, his poor little cheeks cherry red.

"How is he doing?" she whispered, placing a reassuring hand on Henry's shoulder.

"We just got back here," Henry said, growling in frustration. "We haven't even been given a room, much less seen a doctor yet. Apparently hives covering a baby's skin doesn't rank very high on their scale of how serious an illness this may be."

"Try to relax, sweetie. They are seeing him now, and that's what's important."

The nurse checking over Levi met Charli's gaze and smiled calmly. "We had an emergency come in through an ambulance," she explained in a patient tone. "A code blue. As hard as it is to wait, these situations happen sometimes. Please don't worry. We'll be taking care of sweet little Levi here as soon as possible. You brought him to the right place."

Poor Henry didn't want to hear the nurse's words and was scowling and grumbling under his breath, but what the nurse said made sense to Charli. She was certain if Levi was having trouble breathing or anything more serious, he would have been seen sooner rather than later. And if there was any change to his condition, they were right here at the hospital where they could have instant assistance if necessary.

"He has a bit of a fever. One-hundred-and-three-point-five," the nurse continued. "His heart and lungs sound good."

"He has a fever of one-hundred-and-three-point-five? What does that mean? That sounds really high," Henry pressed.

"I'll take you back to an exam room and then bring him some acetaminophen to bring down the fever," the nurse assured him. "Babies often have higher fevers than adults when they've got something else going on as well. The doctor will be able to tell you more once they have a look at him."

The nurse led them to a tiny curtained-off room and handed Charli a TV remote to an equally small TV hung in one corner as Henry crawled onto the bed, still cuddling Levi close to his chest.

"Not many choices on the television, I'm afraid," the triage nurse said before leaving the room.

"She thinks we're going to want to watch TV?" Henry croaked, then growled in frustration.

"I think for some people, watching a show will take their minds off their troubles."

"Not me," he said, his voice gravelly.

"No," she agreed. She set the remote aside.

The hospital registrar came in, asking about insurance.

Henry blanched. "I've only had Levi for a few days," he explained.

The registrar's gaze narrowed on the baby, who was clearly more than just a few days old. "I'm sorry?"

"My sister. She—" Henry started, but Charli cut in.

"Levi is Henry's nephew. We're currently seeking guardianship," she explained.

"I see. Where are his parents?"

"Dad is unknown. We don't know where Levi's mom is."

"That may be problematic."

"How so?" Charli pressed.

"Only legal parents or guardians are allowed to bring in babies."

"Like I said, we're in the process of seeking legal guardianship. Our court date is coming up in about a month or so, and then of course we'll get Levi on health insurance right away. I have all his paperwork here. His birth certificate, our court date, everything."

"You're Henry's wife?" the registrar queried.

Charli tensed, realizing her answer was only going to

make things even more complicated, which was the last thing she wanted.

"His fiancée," she said, flashing her engagement ring at the registrar. "We plan to marry soon."

"I see," the registrar said again. In Charli's opinion, she didn't sound as if she *saw* anything, and Henry was looking as if he might detonate at any moment, so Charli pushed harder.

"Surely the hospital has some policy on not being able to turn away anyone in need of medical assistance." She pressed the folder containing Levi's legal documents into the registrar's hand. "Check with your supervisor, please."

"I'll do that," the registrar agreed. "I'll bring back your documents once I've made copies."

The registrar left the room, and Charli let out a breath she hadn't even realized she'd been holding.

Henry pulled Levi tightly to him and gave Charli a strained smile. "Thank you," he said, his voice low and hoarse. "I don't know what I would have done if you hadn't been here. If you hadn't thought to bring his legal documents."

"I'm convinced it was a God thing," she said. "I was halfway out the door when I felt an inner prompting to grab that folder from my office."

"I'm grateful to God, too, of course, although I'll feel better after we know what's going on with Levi."

"Yeah, me, too. Hopefully it's nothing major." Charli sat down in the chair next to the bed where Henry was perched with the baby in his arms. She reached out and touched his biceps, feeling the muscle twinge beneath her grasp. "We'll get through this," she promised him. "Together."

* * *

Henry had never been so worried in his entire life. From the moment Levi woke up screaming with a cry Henry hadn't heard before and hadn't recognized to waiting in a small ER exam room for the doctor to come, this nightmare had been getting worse and worse. He wasn't kidding when he said he didn't know what he would have done without Charli by his side. He'd been amazed at the way she'd stood up to the registrar, who'd finally conceded to their right to have Levi seen.

Once they'd gotten legal guardianship, he'd immediately need to look into getting health insurance for Levi. Yet another item he'd have to add to his ever-growing list of things to do. Having a baby was so much more complicated than he would ever have imagined.

"One crisis at a time," Charli said, as if she'd been reading his mind. "Stay focused. Keep breathing."

A nurse came in and repeated the baby's vitals, then offered Levi a dropperful of grape acetaminophen. The baby made a funny face and then repeatedly licked at the dropper. Despite the circumstances, Henry smiled softly at the sheer cuteness of the moment.

"I'll have to remember he likes the grape flavor," he said, stroking the dark hair off Levi's warm forehead. "Isn't that right, little guy?"

He felt as if they waited forever before a doctor finally entered the room. If he even was a real doctor. In Henry's mind, the young man didn't look old enough to hold such credentials, and that only made Henry feel far more than his thirty-six years. How many years did it take to get through medical school? Or were they handing out medical licenses to kindergarteners these days?

"Let's have a look at the little guy," the doctor announced, then started a thorough head to toe examination, including looking at his eyes and inside his ears, which made Levi squirm, and then listening to his heart, tummy and breathing. "Hmm," he said after a minute. "Do the hives seem to bother him? Is he acting as if they are itchy at all?"

Henry had to think about the answer to that question. "I don't really know," he answered. "He was screaming in discomfort, but I don't know if it was from the hives or not. That said, the rash looks horrible. Should I have used some calamine lotion on him or something?"

The doctor chuckled. "Not unless you're looking to make him into a pumpkin. No, seriously. As far as I can tell, he doesn't appear to be bothered by the hives."

"So they are hives, then?" Charli questioned.

"Yes. Quite typical, in fact. We see these all the time in the ER in babies around Levi's age."

"You do?" Henry let out a sigh of relief. "What are they from? And how do we treat him, then, if not with calamine?"

"This may come as a surprise to you, but I recommend pain numbing gel for his gums," the doctor answered promptly. "Get the infant kind. And maybe a frozen teething toy or two. He's cutting his first teeth. That's what's causing the rash."

"Really?" Henry and Charli said at the same time.

"Really," the doctor assured them, nodding.

"Which teeth?" Charli asked curiously.

"Bottom front two," the doctor answered with a smile. "You can feel the bumps if you rub your finger against his gums."

"Won't that hurt him to touch his gums?" Henry asked, reaching for Charli's hand as she started to move forward to do just what the doctor had suggested.

"Not at all," the doctor assured him. "Actually, it's the opposite. If anything, a little pressure will feel good to the little guy."

Henry took his hand away from Charli's and allowed her to rub her finger on Levi's gums.

"I can feel them!" she said excitedly. "I can't believe he's teething already. How long will it be until they break through?"

"It's hard to say for sure, but probably within the next couple of days," the doctor answered. "And then he'll feel so much better."

"But you're sure that's all it is?" Henry asked. Could it really be something that simple? "It's not something more serious?" Henry already knew the answer. He could see it in the way Charli had relaxed. But he still wanted to hear it out of the doctor's mouth.

"It may feel like something major over the next couple of days until the teeth break through. Levi may be fussy and uncomfortable, and he may continue to run a bit of a fever. Use infant acetaminophen as directed on the box and the numbing gel and teething toys as needed. He'll be back to his cheery self before you know it."

"*Grape* acetaminophen," Henry said, kissing Levi's soft cheek. "He likes grape flavor."

"Does he now?" the doctor said. "It's fun when babies start showing their preferences and discover the world. My youngest only likes cherry flavor. Wait until you start feeding solids in earnest. You'll either have it be about him not being able to get enough bananas, or he'll spit shirt-staining carrots right back at you."

Henry appreciated that the doctor was trying to make him feel better, but it wasn't working. He was still in knots over all this, remembering how helpless he'd felt when he'd discovered Levi covered in spots.

"And the hives?" Charli asked, picking up on Henry's next question before he could vocalize it himself. "What do we need to do about those? Antibiotics?"

"They'll fade on their own, but they may last a week to ten days. If they get any worse or it starts to appear as if they're bothering him, bring him back here or to his regular pediatrician for a follow-up appointment. They aren't bacterial, so an antibiotic wouldn't do any good."

A regular pediatrician. Yet another item Henry hadn't even considered until this moment. The list was getting awfully long, and fast. He pulled out his cell phone.

"Bored already? Scrolling through social media? Or are you going to post a photo of Levi with a rash?" Charli teased with the first genuine smile she'd given him since they'd arrived at the hospital. They'd both been stressed to the limit, and the collective exhale after finding out Levi's hives were no more serious than a bout of teething had affected them both.

"I'm not going to post pictures of Levi on social media," he assured her.

"Of course not," she agreed. "You're going to be a good daddy that way."

His skin danced with goose bumps.

Daddy?

Would he ever be ready for that title? It seemed far too out there for him to earn, especially from where he was now.

"Levi is a cute little thing," he said, "but even if I wanted to post pictures, I don't have any social media accounts."

"Now, why doesn't that surprise me?" She chuckled.

He narrowed his gaze on her. Was she giving him a hard time?

"Who has time to scroll?" he scoffed. Truth be told, he didn't even carry his cell phone around most of the time. He'd never seen the point, except as a way to communicate with Charli and her father when they were out on the far fields.

Now he would need to be on call 24/7.

"If you must know, I've been down the rabbit hole of scrolling from time to time. I keep up with college friends that way."

"Really? I've never seen you on your phone unless it's for work," he said.

"I'm sneaky. But seriously, that's something that you'll have to work out as a new daddy. You'll always need to be available for Levi's carers. Yet another decision to consider."

There was that word again, as if Charli had already worked it all out in her mind. He wondered if she'd tried on the *Mama* moniker for herself yet. He almost threw the question at her, then thought better of it.

"That's actually what I was about to ask you," he said instead.

She raised her brows. "Which social media platform do I think is best to post your cutie on?"

"If I was going to friend anyone, it would be you," he admitted. "But no. What I really wanted to ask is what app you use to create your lists." Charli was a consummate list maker. This much he knew was true. And though he'd never seen her scrolling through social media, he'd definitely seen her consult her cell phone any number of times over the years to keep track of things, especially ever since she'd taken over most of the business side of running the Stafford ranch. Lists and spreadsheets put her in her happy zone.

He'd never thought he'd be the type to use a phone app for anything. He was the laid-back ranch hand who almost always did things by instinct. But his gut feelings weren't going to help him where raising a baby was concerned, as he was learning with every day that passed.

Since he hoped to become Levi's guardian, he had a lot of new things to learn. And that included how to use his phone beyond texting or making a call.

"I have a couple of notetaking apps I employ regularly. It depends on what features you want to use. Are you looking to create a list on this phone to help you not forget dates, like when Levi has a doctor's appointment, or an alarm for when you need to quit for the day in order to retrieve him from day care?"

His head started to throb again. He hadn't even thought of those things. And she believed he was going to handle this *Daddy* thing with any kind of success? It was all he could do to be a good ranch hand. Fatherhood was something else entirely.

Daddy. The word echoed through his aching mind.

"Well, yes, I guess I do. But I was actually thinking about some kind of note app to use. You know, like to make a list of things I need to pick up at the grocery store? I have a bunch of stuff I need to remember."

"Right." She rattled off a couple of her favorite list-making apps. "You can try each of them out and decide which one you like the best. Then use your calendar app for appointments and your clock to set alarms."

This was far more than he was ready to deal with.

"Remember, no matter how complicated it gets, we've got this. God won't give us more than we can handle," she said, once again appearing to read his mind.

What was up with this woman?

Then her words penetrated, and his heart clenched. She'd said *us*.

Chapter Seven

"That should do it," Charli said, pushing Enter on her desktop computer keyboard in her office. Having a knack for numbers, she'd done all the accounting and other paperwork for the ranch for years, but this was different. She was seated at the desk, and Henry stood with his hand on the back of her chair, leaning over her shoulder and reading the screen from behind her. Levi was soundly napping in a playpen they'd installed in her office a few days ago for times like today when she and Henry were mostly working inside. Charli thought his little snore in the background was adorable, something between a soft bumblebee buzz and a sigh.

They'd just finished submitting their application for Levi's legal guardianship. Now all they had to do was wait for their court date, when they'd have the opportunity to plead their case as to why they should become Levi's official guardians and eventually parents.

It had to happen, and Charli was praying nonstop for a good outcome. Yet she was still struggling with the notion of becoming a mother, even knowing it was the right thing to do for all concerned.

The *only* thing to do.

It didn't matter that Levi had suddenly arrived in their

lives, or that until that moment she hadn't even thought about becoming a wife, much less a mother. She supposed she'd have eventually settled down with a husband and children, but even that was more of a practical thing than anything romantic. She'd pictured a partner with whom she would share her life and work rather than any kind of Disney prince riding up on a white stallion and sweeping her away.

And now she had what she wanted—a permanent partner she could actually trust—pretty much wrapped up and handed to her with a neat little bow. But she had other problems to consider now. Martha pressuring her to sell the ranch was enough in itself, even without her new commitment to Henry and the baby, but at the end of the day, Levi's needs won out even against her own. He, and by extension Henry, were now her number one priorities.

She already knew Henry would be a wonderful father, so she'd just have to deal with her own fears about being a good mom the best she was able. Could she really be the kind of mother Levi needed? She honestly didn't know. She'd never had a role model from whom to learn, and that scared her silly. She'd always considered herself a strong, independent woman, but now she wasn't so sure.

She gathered her papers into a file and straightened her desk. "Are you ready to face down the dragon?" she asked without mirth, only half serious about her joke. Her mother's no-nonsense attitude wasn't easy for her to deal with, especially because Martha was threatening to take away everything she loved.

"Don't you mean *dragons*, plural?" His hand moved to rest on her shoulder, giving it a compassionate squeeze. "Don't forget—I've met Martha and Cordelia."

"True, that," she agreed.

"That said, I don't think it's as bad as you may imagine it is," he commented, though Charli didn't think he sounded as if he really meant it. "It may not seem like it now, but I believe your mom wants what's best for you."

"Yeah. She just has a totally different idea of what *best for me* is. She doesn't see me as a rancher."

"You'll convince her."

Charli wished she believed that, but she wasn't sure she did. So far, all her discussions with her mom and sisters had been less than productive, with the possible exception of Fiona, who'd reached out to help with the baby and appeared to want to let bygones be bygones. They'd been so young when their parents had split. It wasn't her fault, nor was it her sisters', that there was an enormous rift between them.

Still, she wasn't quite certain she trusted Fiona, with her happy-go-lucky temperament. Did anyone truly act like that? Charli had never been the type to see the glass half full, and bouncy personalities annoyed her. Henry appeared to like her though, and they didn't have a more convenient situation for watching the baby while they were out working the ranch. Fiona was a godsend in that regard. Besides, it was only temporary, while they worked out all the details. Eventually, maybe after she and Henry had tied the knot, they'd have to hire a nanny to watch Levi on a more permanent basis.

"I hope I can show them who I really am, but I'm not as confident as you are going into this. I don't really know the best way to present what I've worked out for them. I already know they don't care how I feel about the ranch one way or the other. They're only thinking about selling the ranch and what they'll get out of it. I can see the dollar signs in their eyes. Like those cartoons. *Cha-ching.* But I've worked it out, and the numbers are in their favor—if they'll actually listen to me."

"They will." Henry scooped Levi from the playpen. "Let's do this."

"Ring on my finger? Check. Armed with financials? Check. Okay, then. I can't put this off any longer."

Charli was impressed by how easily Henry threaded the baby into the carrier sling wrap. She was still working that contraption out and couldn't have done it in twice the time it had taken Henry. She always felt as if she was wrapping poor Levi in knots when she tried to sling him to her front.

"You're getting good at that thing," she said with a grin.

"Huh. I should be."

"Yeah?" She crossed her arms. "Why is that?"

"I practiced taking him in and out of the sling a couple dozen times until I got the hang of it," he admitted. "I don't think he liked the exercise very much and he complained a lot when I was trying to work it out, but now I'm confident in the process, so it'll benefit him in the long run."

"Cheater," she teased.

"How is that cheating? I just don't want to be embarrassed because I'm fiddling around with the sling all the time, making a big mess of it while Levi is screaming his head off in distress."

Charli scoffed. "The way I do, you mean."

"What? Fiddling around with the sling or screaming in distress?"

"Ha ha. Very funny."

He flashed her a crooked grin. "I try."

"What?" She chuckled and shook her head. "To humiliate me?"

"No, not at all. You are good at so many things. Give me this one win, at least."

"Indeed. You are officially proclaimed King of the Baby Sling," she pronounced, rolling her hands as she gave him a mock bow.

They'd always had this easy camaraderie between them in the past, and she was glad they were still friendly even though they were now engaged and everything else between them had changed. She wondered if they'd continue with this easy dynamic once they were married.

Would a wedding change everything?

Henry felt as if he was in some kind of dream. Was he really engaged to the beautiful, smart, kind woman walking beside him? He wanted to pinch himself.

He still wasn't entirely sure how this had happened. A ranch. A family. And most of all, Charli. It was as if God had reached into his heart and granted his every desire. So why did he feel so awkward about it all?

He glanced toward her. She looked worried, and no wonder. Her whole future banked on how this meeting with her mom and sisters went. Yet despite everything, she had a determined set to her jaw and held her shoulders stiff and straight.

Maybe a little bit too stiff, he observed as he flashed her another sidelong glance.

He stopped and looked around, noticing the blooming multicolored wildflowers and looking for one type of yellow bloom in particular, the evening primrose, which Henry knew was Charli's favorite flower. Spotting one not far from the well-trodden dirt path, he wrapped an arm firmly around Levi, who was snug and sound asleep in his carrier, and carefully crouched, snapping the stem just under the bloom.

He turned toward Charli, calling her name. "Hold up just a second."

Before he could think better of it, he approached her and tucked the yellow flower behind her left ear, gently leaning down and kissing her cheek. "Trust God. He'll work everything out."

Shock and confusion crossed her expression, and her mouth worked, though at first no sound emerged.

"Henry, I..." she said at last.

Not wanting to hear what she was going to say, Henry swiveled on the toes of his boots and strode forward a few steps before stopping to let Charli catch up.

Worse than expecting her to call him out on doing something stupid and romantic, both of which were true, he'd been even more terrified in that moment that he'd blurt out, "Beauty for a beauty," or something equally as inane. He knew better than to do that. Offering her a flower at all was pushing the envelope as it was.

"Why did you do that?" she asked quietly, her whispered voice cracking with strain. She stared at him with her wide-eyed blue gaze, a palm over the spot where his lips had brushed her cheek.

"No reason."

Charli stopped and reached for Henry's arm. "Henry, you know you don't have to prove anythi—"

"Yeah," he said, jumping in before she could finish her

sentence. "It's no big deal. Yellow primroses are your favorite flowers, right?"

"How do you know that?"

"What?" His heart pounded. Had he made a mistake? "You don't like yellow primroses best?"

"No—yes. They're my favorite flower. But I'm surprised you knew. I don't ever remember telling you that. So how did you guess?"

Henry's face heated. How was he supposed to answer *that* question without giving himself away?

That he always kept an eye on her, protecting her even when she wasn't aware of it?

That his gaze was never far from her whenever they were working together in the fields or in the office?

That he'd made it a point to know as much about her as he could—everything from her favorite meal, which was steak grilled medium rare with steamed artichokes dipped in mayonnaise, to her favorite type of music, which was Irish folk music, to her favorite flower, the yellow primrose.

He studied her as if she was precious artwork made directly by God, because to Henry, that was exactly who she was.

"I feel as if we need to talk about this," she said, her voice low and sober.

Henry shook his head. That was the last thing he wanted to do. Words didn't come easy to him, and when he tried to speak with actions from his heart without using words, he ended up in situations like this one.

"We really don't," he assured her. "It's no big deal."

It was just a flower. And clearly, it had been a mistake. And the kiss?

He definitely didn't want to go there.

When was he going to learn to think before he acted?

"I disagree," Charli pressed, her brow furrowed. "But I don't have the time or emotional bandwidth to deal with this right now. I have too much on my mind already."

"I know you do."

She sighed. "Let's pick this up later."

They'd reached the main house, and as if they'd silently agreed to do so in advance, they both stopped and faced each other.

Charli inhaled deeply and held out her hand to him. She flashed him what he thought must be her best version of a smile, though at the moment it looked more like a painful grimace than anything.

"Okay," she said on a sigh. "Let's go. I can't put this off any longer."

Chapter Eight

Charli was gripping Henry's hand so tightly she was certain she must be cutting off his circulation, but when she met his gaze, she saw nothing but strength and compassion for her. His stunning blue eyes glowed with intensity, and her breath hitched in her throat. She didn't know how things had gotten to the point they now were, but she had to wonder why she'd never seen Henry for the incredible man he was until she'd needed his help. How had she worked with him every day and not noticed what a good-looking cowboy he was? If her father hadn't passed away and left her in this dire situation with the ranch, would she ever have perceived Henry as more than a friend?

She didn't know, and though the idea was mind-blowing, now wasn't the time to ponder the thought.

Her mom and sisters were already gathered in the living room when she and Henry entered the house. Though they were all staying in guest rooms at the ranch house, Charli's room was down a different hallway, and she had mostly managed to avoid them. She was up at dawn every day and out of the house long before her relatives woke, and she ate her meals with Henry and Levi, so when she returned to the main house in the evenings, she went straight to her bedroom and locked the door behind her.

Today, however, she couldn't avoid these women who were her blood kin and yet virtual strangers to her.

Lord, give me the right words to make my case. And give my sisters open hearts to help them see the truth.

Maybe it wasn't fair for her to think that way. She was praying that her sisters would see things her way, yet her father had clearly had a higher purpose in writing his will the way he had, a purpose she could hardly bear to consider. Maybe she was being selfish in trying to keep the ranch. But she had to try, because surely her father hadn't meant for her to do something different with her life than living the way she'd been raised. He of all people had known how much she loved the ranch.

What had he said in his letter?

Love will find a way.

But how?

What did you mean, Daddy?

But it didn't matter how often she'd gone over her father's cryptic words in her mind; she couldn't figure it out.

Dropping Henry's hand, she perched straight-backed on the right edge of the evergreen love seat. Henry unfastened Levi from his sling, and Charli held the baby for a moment while Henry rummaged through the diaper bag for a bottle. He settled down next to her, leaning back into the cushions and looking far more relaxed and comfortable than she knew he really felt as he took his nephew back into his arms and pressed the bottle into his mouth.

Despite the gnawing in her stomach, she smiled softly at the man so gently caring for his nephew. For as much as he'd said he had no idea what he was doing with a baby, he certainly looked the part of a doting uncle.

"So, then. When are you getting married?" Cordelia asked, sounding more than a little suspicious. "Have you talked about it yet?"

"We, er..." Charli stumbled.

"We haven't set a date yet," Henry answered for her. "But given the circumstances, it'll likely be sooner rather than later. We have no reason to wait."

Martha, Fiona and Cordelia all sat wide-eyed and silent as they observed Charli's little family. She hoped the scene was having the kind of positive influence she and Henry were going for. If her sisters didn't end up being generous with her for her own sake—and honestly, there was no reason for them to be, she acknowledged, since they didn't know her any better than she knew them—at least hopefully they would consider the baby and realize just how much the ranch would mean for Levi's future.

She'd spent last night thinking about how she'd act and what she'd say when the moment arrived, so the first thing she did was lay her left hand—the one with Henry's grandmother's beautiful ring glittering from it—palm down on top of the file folders in her lap. She was gratified by Cordelia's pleasant gasp of surprise. She wasn't nearly as happy when she observed the sardonic twist of Martha's lips, but she was already in for a penny, in for a pound. If she couldn't convince her mother of the rightness of her proposition, it would all be for naught.

There would be no going back now.

Charli took a deep breath and caught her mother's eye, raising her eyebrows in question. The scene felt eerily similar to the first time they'd met together in this room to talk about their futures, but this time she was prepared for what was to come and wasn't going to be knocked for a loop by her relatives. She prayed the Lord would touch her mother's and sisters' hearts, with a positive outcome for all.

Martha leaned forward and brushed a stray curl of her short auburn hair behind her right ear. Her gaze remained locked on Charli's. Surprisingly, Charli didn't see bitterness or anger in her mother's eyes, both of which she had half expected, fairly or unfairly, might be there. But she did see the reflection of her own determination in her mother's blue-eyed depths, and she suddenly felt an odd kinship with her.

Maybe she was more like her mother than she'd originally thought. The feeling unnerved her. She'd always believed she was her father's daughter through and through.

She broke eye contact with Martha and glanced at her sisters. Cordelia appeared every bit as stiff as Charli felt, sitting on the couch next to her mother with her back ramrod straight, her arms defensively crossed in front of her and a frown on her face. Fiona, in contrast, was smiling and appeared totally relaxed in the fluffy chocolate-colored armchair, with her legs tucked up cross-legged and her chin resting in her cupped palms.

Charli waited, but no one started what was clearly going to be a tricky conversation, and the silence in the room was painfully deafening, excruciating in more ways than one. It was almost a physical experience—gut-wrenching, as if someone had reached a fist inside her belly and then clenched and twisted. And as if that wasn't enough, everyone's heated gaze was on her, sharply darting into her. Her skin prickled as she cleared her throat, lifted her chin and forced her expression into neutrality in a vain attempt to keep from showing how uncomfortable she felt inside.

Henry laid the now-sleeping Levi on a blanket next to

his feet, which had the added benefit of unconsciously causing everyone to momentarily shift their focus and look at the precious napping baby. Charli took a deep breath, relaxing into Henry when he put his arm around her shoulders, pulling her into the strength of his chest.

"You guys," Fiona gushed. "I know I've said this before, but your baby is so cute. I can't stand it."

Your baby.

Charli internalized the words even as she let the comment pass, while Henry mumbled his thanks and agreement.

"Since we've all been staying at the ranch," Fiona continued, "I've been using this time to relax and vacation. I've been exploring your property and taking hikes every morning. It's truly lovely."

Charli raised her eyebrows, surprised that not only did Fiona appear to be enjoying her time in the Montana mountains, but that she'd referred to the ranch as Charli's property. Could it really be that easy? If Fiona was already on their side, they could very well be winning half the battle.

"Thank you," Charli said, offering Fiona a tentative smile. "This land is my heartbeat. It's my whole life, and I can't imagine living anywhere else."

"The land is beautiful, but I have to admit I'm mostly drawn to the animals. I spent quite a bit of time watching your herd of horses frolicking out in the field, nudging and bucking and playing with each other. But even more than those gorgeous horses, your cows are just too cute," Fiona continued. "I couldn't get enough of them. I've never seen shaggy cows before, not even in pictures or on television. Absolutely adorable!"

Charli had never considered her cows *cute* before, even when she'd first brought in the Highland cattle she'd used to crossbreed with her Herefords to strengthen her herd's genetic makeup. In her mind, cattle meant business, and she'd never once considered how they looked beyond being healthy, well-built and prolific producers.

What, she wondered, did that say about her as a woman?

Did she even have a feminine heart at all if she was consistently missing the obvious right in front of her eyes? If she looked at the Highland cattle through Fiona's eyes, she supposed they were cute.

And the cows weren't the only things she'd been oblivious to. She hadn't often considered getting married and starting a family, either. She'd never been the type of woman who dreamed about two-point-five kids, a white picket fence and a dog, other than her herding pups that made her life easier. Even the Kelpies would look strange to a woman like Fiona who would view them as pets. Working dogs stayed with the herd or in their outside kennels, not in the house. A relationship just hadn't been on her radar until her father had died and left her in this mess she wouldn't be able to get out of without Henry's help. It was as if she'd been wearing blinders. She'd been working side by side with Henry for many years and somehow hadn't recognized how magnificent he was both inside and out.

Henry getting down on one knee and presenting her with an engagement ring after they were already technically engaged, not to mention the way he'd given her that flower this morning with the sweetest, gentlest of kisses had made her incredibly uncomfortable in all the wrong ways. And now she was faced with the realization that she'd never considered her own cows to be *cute* when, at face value and probably to most women, at least, they really were.

"The shaggy ones are called Highland cows," Charli explained when everyone continued to stare in her direction as if waiting for an answer.

"Like from Scotland?" Fiona put a hand over her heart. "I've always wanted to visit Scotland. It's on my bucket list."

Charli couldn't help but laugh. "Well, I didn't buy them directly from Scotland. After doing some research on the breed and talking with some nearby ranchers, we purchased ours from a neighbor's stock. But yes, originally Highland cows were bred in Scotland. The land up in the Highlands is rougher than here in Montana, and they've grown to be a strong, hardy breed that offers a lot to intermix with my own Hereford stock."

"Would it be okay if I—I mean, could I maybe pet one?" Fiona asked tentatively, clasping her hands in front of her, her eyes glittering with excitement.

Pet a cow?

Seriously? Did she mean the same way she'd scratch a dog or a cat under the chin or rub it between the ears?

That was so far away from Charli's daily existence she couldn't even imagine it. But she supposed looking at it from Fiona's 100 percent *non*ranching background, animals were animals, and she'd already voiced that she thought the Highland cows were cute. So following the idea to its logical conclusion, she supposed in Fiona's mind, at least, petting a cow wasn't such a strange notion.

"Sure you can," Henry answered before Charli could even wrap her mind around Fiona's request, much less answer. His voice sounded nearly as upbeat as Fiona's.

"We'd be happy to take you out to meet our herd and introduce you to all the horses and cattle."

"Eww." This comment was from Cordelia, whose expression appeared as grossed out as Fiona's had looked eager.

"I'm sorry?" Charli questioned. As odd as Fiona's request had appeared, *no one* dissed her cattle.

"I think cows are disgusting. How can you say they're cute, Fiona? They lick their noses! You can count me out of that little excursion."

Henry actually chuckled. "So maybe cows aren't your thing, Cordelia. What about horses? Are they more your style? We could set up a group trail ride for everyone and show you all our land."

Charli thought that was an especially clever spur of the moment idea. Martha was already well acquainted with the ranch from her past, but her sisters weren't.

Cordelia was already firmly shaking her head, but to Charli's surprise, Martha chose then to speak up.

"Trail riding on horseback through these beautiful mountains is maybe the one and only thing I miss about this miserable little town. Don't turn such a wonderful experience down too quickly, Cordelia. At least give it some thought. Trust me. I think you'll like it more than you expect."

Before Cordelia could entirely nix the idea, Henry roped in the deal. "Consider it done. I'll plan our outing and let you know when and where. Don't worry, Cordelia. I promise we've got the best, gentlest horses. You'll love it."

Charli didn't miss the expression that crossed Cordelia's face, and to her surprise, it wasn't disgust—it was fear. She tucked that information in the back of her mind for later. When the day of the trail ride came, it would be critical for Cordelia to bond with her mount.

She tried to make eye contact with Henry, but his attention was on her family. Though she trusted him, she wasn't immediately sure where Henry was going with showing the cattle to Fiona. Maybe he was thinking they'd be showing off their ranch?

Their ranch?

That concept was still hard for her to wrap her mind around, but she knew she needed to embrace that truth. He was definitely stepping up, making it appear as if he and Charli were a legitimate couple—which she supposed, in the oddest of ways, they were.

Legitimate. But not even close to real.

"As much as I've enjoyed our conversation so far, I think we need to regroup. We're here to talk about the will," Charli reminded everyone. From the tension in her shoulders, Henry could tell Charli was tired of all the small talk about cute cows and trail rides when her entire livelihood was on the line. He imagined she probably couldn't think about anything else until this was solved.

Martha nodded. "Among other things, yes."

He wondered what *other things* Martha could be referring to, but he remained quiet.

Charli reached into the top file folder on her lap and withdrew a stack of spreadsheets. "I've already crunched the numbers, so I'll start."

"No," her mother interrupted in a clipped tone.

Henry's fight response was instantly triggered when Charli's shoulders tightened even more. He was usually laid-back and not much got to him, but right now every masculine instinct within him raged to protect Charli from her hostile relatives. His nerves snapped with adrenaline, and he crossed his arms and hid his fisted hands behind his biceps, knowing that stepping in now would only make things worse. He was here in a support role. That was his part of the marriage bargain. This had become his fight when he'd put his grandmother's ring on Charli's finger, but he doubted Charli would want him to step in. Not just yet anyway.

"We already know your pitch," Martha said in a monotone. "You don't need to present us with a PowerPoint or anything to try to represent your thoughts on the matter. You want to keep the ranch, but it's not clear in your father's will how exactly you expect that to happen."

That was harsh, especially coming from Martha. While there hadn't been much communication between Charli and her mother over the years, he would have expected more from her than that.

"We know what the will says since we met with the lawyer. What I'd like to hear—and I want *you* to hear—is what your sisters have to say about their own hopes for their futures," Martha continued.

Henry clenched his jaw. What Martha really meant was she wanted to highlight why Fiona and Cordelia wanted to sell the ranch, take the money and run away with it.

"Okay," Charli agreed, sounding doubtful. "I'm listening."

"Fiona? What do you plan to do with the money you'll receive from the sale of the ranch as we learned when the will was read?"

Henry's breath punched into his lungs. He didn't miss

the way Martha used the present tense. Not *the money you might receive* but *the money you will receive*.

To her credit, Fiona's eyes widened, and she appeared concerned. "We haven't made any definite plans as to what will happen with the will," she reminded her mother. "And so I haven't planned anything individually, either. I'd think we need to talk about different options first."

"Don't tell me you haven't been thinking about the future," Martha pressed. "You're too much of a dreamer for me to believe that."

"No, I didn't say that. The truth is, I've fallen in love with this area while I've been here, and I don't especially have anything worthwhile to go home to. I may decide to make Hope my home."

Charli threaded her fingers through Henry's, squeezing hard. He wondered if anyone else had noticed the way her breathing had increased. He rubbed the back of her hand with his palm, silently communicating with her.

"I'm not sure exactly what I have in mind yet, but I'm thinking about doing something in the hospitality industry, maybe, since that's what I'm trained in and what I was doing back in Denver. I imagine this may be a very good area for that."

"Fiona is a much sought after event planner in Colorado," Cordelia cut in, beaming at her sister. It was the first time Henry had seen Cordelia smile and was amazed at how it changed her countenance. "She runs her own company. We're all proud of her."

"That's fantastic," Charli said, smiling tightly at Fiona. No one except Henry would probably notice the way her throat had squeezed around the words.

"But Fiona—you can't seriously be considering making Hope your home," Martha said. "You won't find nearly the number and quality of clientele you have ripe for the picking in your company in Denver."

"I get that. So maybe not in the same way," Fiona agreed cheerfully. Henry didn't think he'd ever met a person with a more glass-half-full attitude than Fiona. "I'll probably have to pivot to make it work. But I've spent the last ten years doing nothing but focusing on my career nonstop. I've hardly had any time for a social life and just to relax a bit. I think it's time for me to slow down and enjoy my life for a change. What better place to find a real sense of peace than a nice country inn?"

"Honey, I think you need to think this through more carefully," Martha cautioned. "I grew up in this wretched little town. Trust me. Adorable cows and cute country boys will get old fast. If you've burned your bridges in Denver, what will you do then?"

Fiona shrugged. "I've thought about that. But what's my life ever going to amount to if I never take a risk?"

Martha had attractive laugh lines around her eyes, but now Henry observed frown lines forming and thought she should smile more often. In that way Charli followed after her mom, frequently too serious and not laughing enough. That was one way he hoped his partnership with Charli would benefit her and ease her burden, give her more reasons to smile.

Martha paused a moment to absorb Fiona's opinion, which she clearly hadn't expected, before scoffing softly and turning her attention to Cordelia. "What about you? I know you're not enamored of country life."

"Not even close," Cordelia assured her. "I'm so grateful you raised me in the city. I definitely belong there.

Unlike Fiona, however, I don't have a job to go back to, and that's going to be problematic."

"What?" Martha said, clearly shocked by the revelation. "Why is this the first time I'm hearing about this?"

Cordelia's face reddened, and she shifted in her seat, clasping her hands in her lap and staring at them as if they'd provide answers.

Finally, she cleared her throat. "Matt and I broke up," Cordelia admitted, sounding miserable.

"Humph. Well, I have to admit that's no surprise," Martha said bluntly. "I told you he was bad news from the beginning."

"Don't remind me. And he didn't just break up with me. He fired me," Cordelia continued. "So I have no job to go back to, and no boyfriend to tie me there."

"I warned you. Didn't I tell you? Never get involved with the boss."

"Mama," Fiona said in a gentle reprimand. Then she turned to Cordelia. "Can he even do that? If I were you, I'd speak to human resources."

Cordelia shook her head. "I thought about it, but I wouldn't want to stay even if I could. It does, however, put me in an awkward situation."

Henry slid a glance at Charli to see how she was taking all this news. Cordelia was obviously hurting, but it was equally apparent to Henry that she was as stubborn as a goat, much as Charli was. Cordelia sounded as if she might not know what was coming up next for her in her life, but he was certain she wouldn't be interested in any of the suggestions Charli may have.

"What if we joined forces and created a bed-and-breakfast together?" Fiona launched out of her chair and plunked down next to Cordelia, taking her hand and squeezing it affectionately. "This could be so much fun. I'll do the bed part, and you can do breakfast. Cordelia went to a famous culinary arts school in Paris," she added, as a way to explain to Henry and Charli why this idea was a particularly good one.

Cordelia didn't look sold on the idea. "I don't see how that would work. I don't do breakfast," she grumbled. "I'm not a morning person."

"Then we'll do dinner instead and sell it to guests as a place to eat and then crash for the night," Fiona said. Henry wondered how far Fiona would push her sister on the idea. It seemed to him as if Cordelia didn't like to be wrangled, especially regarding country living.

"Just think." Fiona held her hands palms outward as if framing a sign. "We could call it the Stafford Sisters Inn. Wouldn't that be lovely?"

Henry narrowed his gaze on Fiona. Did she not realize how insensitive her suggestion would be to Charli? And here he'd thought Fiona was the kind sister. How could she so blatantly leave Charli out of the picture?

He switched his gaze to Charli, but either she hadn't realized Fiona was leaving her out or she didn't care, because the only thing that mattered to her was the ranch and not whether or not she was associated with her sisters. Either way, Henry was relieved. The last thing he wanted was for Charli to feel more pain than she already did.

"While I disagree with having one or both of you stay in Hope, you could use your money from the sale of the ranch as a down payment on some sort of establishment," Martha suggested. "I do like the idea of you girls working together. Or better yet, Fiona, funnel it into your current business in Denver, and Cordie, you can buy a restaurant of your own."

"No," said Fiona. "If we sell the ranch, Charli and her family won't have any place to live. That's not fair to them. We have to come up with a solution that works for all three of us."

"Your father's will specifies that the ranch be sold and the proceeds split between the three of you," Martha reminded her.

"No, it doesn't," Charli protested. Henry breathed a sigh of relief. It was about time she spoke up for herself. For *them*.

"You haven't allowed me to speak yet. I have a proposition for you," Charli continued, finally pulling out the paperwork from her file. "It's less money up front for you, but you'll make more in the long run."

Henry tried to read the pages, but it was all gibberish to him no matter how hard he concentrated. It wasn't just reading he had trouble with. Numbers all swam together—which was why he was a rancher and not an accountant. He was good at caring for animals and land.

"Tell us what you have in mind," Fiona said, encouraging her, though Cordelia and Martha didn't look nearly as interested in Charli's explanation as Henry was hoping.

"For a man who was self-employed, Daddy did very well with his investment portfolio—his stocks, bonds, EFTs. He was always good with numbers. I am willing to split my share of his portfolio between the two of you. That will give you more than enough to do whatever you have your hearts set on. A down payment on an inn if you want, Fiona, or money to build up your business in Denver. And Cordelia? A restaurant, maybe?"

The silence was deafening as the women absorbed what Charli was saying.

"In exchange, you let me and my—" she choked up and couldn't immediately finish her sentence "—my family keep the ranch."

Family.

Henry's stomach flipped in a good way. Despite all the craziness with the will and how exhausted he felt trying to parent Levi, he was feeling overwhelmingly blessed right now in ways he would never have dared ask God for.

"I'm not an accountant, but I don't think that works out evenly," Cordelia protested. "The ranch is worth more than half of Dad's portfolio, isn't it?"

"Yes." Charli didn't even try to hide the truth or disagree with Cordelia's revelation. Henry waited on pins and needles to see what her retort would be, because she clearly had something in mind. "You would make more with the sale of the ranch, at least in the immediate future."

"Then not to put too fine of a point on it, but it's not fair," Cordelia said. "Right?" She looked from Fiona to Martha.

"No, it's not, if you're looking only at today. But I'll also give you a share in the yearly proceeds of the sale of the calves. Five percent for each of you."

Martha tilted her head and narrowed her eyes on Charli. "For how long?"

Charli cleared her throat. "Forever. It will be an investment with permanent dividends. In the long run, you'll make far more than you'd get with the sale of the ranch, and Henry and I will still have our livelihood to depend on."

"That's assuming you have continued successful years," Martha pointed out. "What happens on those years that aren't so great?"

"Lord willing, we will continue to prosper," Charli said without waiting a beat. "God has been good to us." She sounded as if she didn't have a doubt, though there was no way to guarantee a profit on a cow/calf operation, which changed from year to year and depended on many things beyond their control.

"Even if we do have a bad year now and again, you'll still have a positive investment long term. But for us, there's so much more than that. It's not only Henry and me. Levi will have the opportunity to grow up on the ranch and learn what country living is all about."

He was still struggling knowing Charli had offered so much to her sisters, though he knew how desperate she felt to do anything she had to do to keep the ranch.

From the way Cordelia was scrunching her face, it was clear she didn't agree that a ranch was a good place to raise a child, and he already knew how Martha felt about it. She hadn't appreciated growing up in the country. Maybe it wasn't such a good argument, all things considered.

But at the end of the day, only one thing mattered.

Charli had removed her hand from his when she was fumbling through the pages of her proposal, but now he reached out and threaded his fingers though hers again. Maybe they had a way to go to learn how to live and communicate as a couple, sharing all of their lives together. But one thing he did know for certain—

He would support her no matter what.

Chapter Nine

Charli was relieved that her sisters were willing to consider her proposal and not turn it down outright. It wasn't a win, exactly, but at least it wasn't an out-and-out loss as she'd half expected it to be.

Though he hadn't spoken much during the family meeting, Henry had been a huge help to her, supporting her in his usual strong, silent way. Afterward, he'd suggested Fiona accompany them to meet a Highland cow.

Charli still didn't know how she felt about petting cattle. It sounded ridiculous to her, but her sister was certainly thrilled about the prospect. Henry, on the other hand, was acting as if treating cows as pets was an everyday occurrence for him. She let him take the lead, preferring to carry baby Levi tucked in a front sling.

"We're keeping this particular Highland cow in a pen close to the barn so we can watch her, since she's close to giving birth," Henry explained as they walked across the yard. "Just like with humans, the only thing cuter than a mama cow is a baby one. You'll probably get to see the calf if you stay around for a few more days."

It didn't take the three of them long to get to the pen, and once they did, it was clear to Charli that Fiona wouldn't have to stay around even that long for the arrival of the calf.

"You won't even have to wait," Charli told Fiona. She couldn't help but smile at her sister's enthusiasm, marveling again at how different Charli and each of her sisters were. "This cow is in labor right now. If you want to stay and watch, you're about to experience the miracle of birth, cattle style."

"Really?" Fiona exclaimed. "Talk about good timing. What a gift from God! I can't believe it."

Neither could Charli, but she could easily see how this would work in their favor, so maybe the timing really was a gift from God. If she wasn't mistaken, she already had Fiona on her side. Having her sister watch a calf being born was only going to cement her position more firmly in Fiona's mind.

The very pregnant cow mooed loudly in complaint before lying down on the grass and wriggling in discomfort.

"You've got this, girl," Henry said, encouraging the distressed bovine.

"What's the mama cow's name?" Fiona whispered.

"Name?" Charli echoed.

For a cow?

"She doesn't have a name," Henry explained with a chuckle.

"We don't name our cows," said Charli, finding nothing particularly funny about it.

"You don't? Then how do you tell them apart?" Fiona asked curiously.

"We tag their ears with a number," Henry said.

"It doesn't hurt the cows," Charli explained, anticipating Fiona's next question before she could ask it. "We take care to disinfect the area first. It's kind of like getting your ears pierced, I imagine. Just a quick click and it's done."

"Oh." Fiona's eyes widened as the calf began to emerge before them, wiggling its front legs and tossing its head the moment it hit the earth. "Are you going to go in and help?"

"The mama cow doesn't need our help to deliver the calf. We'll give her a few minutes to interact with it, and then I'll go in and check to see if we have a bull calf or a heifer," Henry said.

"This is so exciting," Fiona said as the calf wobbled to its feet on spindly, unsteady legs.

All three of them exclaimed in surprise when the calf took a nosedive and rolled over in an awkward somersault, and then they all laughed when it immediately got back up on its feet again, seemingly no worse for wear.

They watched for a while as the mama took care of her newborn before Henry entered the pen and checked the calf over.

"She's a good mother, already caring for her baby, which is what we like to see. Sometimes the moms reject their calves for whatever reason, and we have to step in and bottle-feed. I don't think we'll have to do that in this case," Charli explained.

Although maybe it wouldn't hurt for Fiona to have the bottle-feeding experience as well, Charli thought in amusement. But then they'd never get her to leave the ranch, much less the town, once she'd experienced bottle-feeding a calf. Charli smothered a laugh at the thought.

"We've got a little bull calf here," Henry announced in his low, rich voice. "Let's see if we can get him to latch on and have his first meal."

"Just like with a human, the initial milk the baby receives is colostrum," Charli explained, "so we try to make certain the calf nurses right away. It's really important that the calf gets the extra vitamins and minerals that the first milk provides, but they don't always instinctively know what they're doing when they're first born, so we often give them a hand to figure it out."

Charli and Fiona watched as Henry expertly guided the calf close to his mother, then coaxed the calf to suck on his fingertips.

"Come on, little guy. Right this way," Henry urged.

"Quite literally, he's giving the calf a hand," Fiona joked with a giggle.

Before long, Henry had transferred the calf's eager lips to his mother and the little bull latched on, the foam lining his mouth a sign that he was getting milk.

Fiona sighed in contentment. After a moment, she spoke. "Okay, I know this is unusual and you two will probably think I'm crazy for even asking, but can I please name these two cows? I promise not to ask you to give names to your whole herd. But getting to see this calf's birth has been amazing, and it's hard for me to think of them now as just *Mama* and *Baby*."

Charli's head was swimming at the notion, which she still couldn't wrap her mind around. She tilted her chin and narrowed her eyes. "What did you have in mind?"

"Well, they'll have to be Scottish names, right? Because they are originally from the Highlands? I was thinking Flossy for the mama cow, and then Finbar for the calf," Fiona said thoughtfully.

Charli couldn't help the laughter that followed, but she

nodded in agreement. "Flossy and Finbar it is. I have to admit those are really cute names."

Yeah. For the cute cows.

And now those names would be forever branded in her mind. She wouldn't be able to look at those two cows again without thinking *Flossy and Finbar*. Hopefully Fiona would keep her promise and stop at naming these two, or else Charli was going to have an entire herd of named cattle running through her mind every time she worked with them, and how confusing would that be?

"Come on into the pen," Henry urged Fiona. "So you can pet Flossy and Finbar." He said the names as if naming cattle was an everyday occurrence at the Stafford ranch. He was certainly taking this whole Fiona shenanigan better than she was. Or maybe he was just a better actor.

Charli watched as Henry guided Fiona forward, suggesting the best way to pet the cows without disturbing Flossy, who was doing her job as mama by carefully watching out for her baby. Charli knew Flossy could be aggressive if she felt any threat to her calf, and she admired the way Henry taught Fiona how to confidently approach Finbar. He was a natural with her sister, another reason to appreciate him for being there with her.

Charli would probably have joined them in the pen, but Levi was tired of being in his sling and was wiggling and fussing to get loose. Quietly shushing him, she removed him from the sling and put him against her shoulder, patting his back in soothing strokes.

"Hush, sweetheart. Your new Daddy is helping your Auntie Fiona learn how to pet our cows." She kissed Levi's soft cheek. It suddenly occurred to her that Levi would be growing up here on the ranch with all the wonderful experiences it offered, assuming her sisters gave them the opportunity. "It won't be long before you're petting the cows, will it?"

She could easily picture a preschool-aged Levi, with the same dark hair and blue eyes as Henry, following him out across the field with Blue at his heels. Of course, Blue wouldn't be a puppy by then, but he'd still be young and rambunctious, and she imagined the dog and the little boy would become good friends.

She remembered her own childhood on the ranch, toddling around her father's heels and learning all there was to know about country living from him. He hadn't just taught her how to do ranch chores, but how to love what she was doing, everything from feeding orphaned calves from a bottle to teaching the dogs herding commands to understanding the business side and keeping the ranch books. It was why she felt so comfortable running the ranch now, despite her mother's doubts about her ability to do so.

Then, when she was a teenager, Daddy had hired Henry as a ranch hand, and he'd worked alongside them. She was only starting to realize it now, but she'd come to depend upon Henry for practically everything. He had the same heart for the country that she and her father had.

And now…now she was going to marry him.

That concept was still hard for her to wrap her mind around, but if she had to get married, there was no one she would rather have as her partner than Henry. She trusted him. And she had to admit he was a physically attractive man. There probably wasn't a woman alive who would turn down one of Henry's smiles.

Levi gurgled as he reached up and patted Charli's hair with his chunky little fists, but it took her a moment to realize he'd grasped the yellow flower Henry had tucked in her hair earlier. Of course, the baby brought it straight to his mouth, and Charli had to move quickly to keep it from reaching his lips.

"No, no, sweetheart. Yucky." She had no idea whether evening primroses were edible or not, but she wasn't about to take a chance.

Not with Henry's baby nephew, who would soon be his son.

Their son, she reminded herself. She was going to be a wife and a mother in the blink of an eye, or at least when she signed her name on the dotted line, first to marry Henry and next for Levi's guardianship and eventual adoption.

It wouldn't be long now.

"You really outdid yourself with the whole *mama and baby cow thing*," Charli told Henry later when they were back at his cabin. She was preparing Levi's bottles for the night, and he was changing the baby's diaper, which oddly enough, he was getting to be an expert at. Even crazier than that was the fact that he didn't mind the chore. It was fun to be able to play with the baby when he was doing diaper duty. Levi was wide awake and interactive when he was getting changed, whereas after he was fed he would curl into Henry's arms and promptly fall asleep. Henry enjoyed that time as well, finding in Levi a sense of contentment he hadn't previously felt in his life.

Henry chuckled as Levi kicked his legs out in unison.

"I am now a cow naming master of ceremonies. Anything I can do to help."

"I don't know about helping, exactly. I'm now going to think of those two as Flossy and Finbar. Good grief. But I suppose it can't hurt, can it?" Charli asked.

"From what I can tell, we've got Fiona solidly locked on our side. She spoke out in your favor when it came to keeping the ranch. I was really proud of you, by the way."

"For what?" she asked, surprised.

"Your proposal. It was brilliant. I couldn't really read it from over your shoulder, but you had it all together, and it made sense to me. Cordelia would be crazy not to take up an offer like that."

She put the newly filled bottles in the refrigerator and turned. Her eyes widened and she covered her mouth with her fingers, shifting uncomfortably under his gaze. "I am so sorry. I'll be honest. It didn't even occur to me to give you a copy of the proposal or explain it to you beforehand. It's always been my father who drafted proposals and made decisions, and now that he's gone, I just took it over myself without giving you the thought you deserved. I forget we're a partnership now. At the very least I should have discussed it with you."

He scooped up Levi, then met Charli's gaze again and saw the truth there. He wasn't fooling anyone. She'd been the one to coach him through his GED. He couldn't read the proposal very well, not because he couldn't see it from where he'd been sitting, but because the numbers and letters became all garbled when he tried to understand them. Giving him a copy of a complicated business document beforehand would only have added to his insecurities as he tried to work through it.

"I don't need a paper copy of stuff. Just a quick verbal run-through would have been fine. Like you said. Discuss it between us. I'm not used to working as partners, either. And you're not wrong trying to split your dad's investments between your sisters so we can keep the ranch. I've gotta say, though, I was surprised you're willing to shave off 10 percent of our yearly earnings for the rest of our lives. That seems like a big commitment."

Her face reddened, and Henry couldn't tell whether it was anger or embarrassment. Her next words didn't help him discern which, either.

"I'm doing the best I can," she snapped.

She was unquestionably defensive now, and Henry wasn't sure how to back off without removing his main point, which was that if she was really going to share the ranch and her life with him, that meant every part of it.

"Look, it's going to take time for us to go from employer and employee to equal partners," she said. "Give me some grace as I learn what that feels like. I'm going to make mistakes."

"As am I. Giving each other grace on a day-by-day basis, moment by moment, even, is a good way to go into our marriage, don't you think?"

Henry sank into the armchair and Charli moved to his side, handing him a bottle for Levi as she pressed a hand to his shoulder. "It's a lot of change in a short time. I'm still having trouble wrapping my mind around the whole thing."

He met her gaze again and saw the struggle written there. He wished he could take it away from her, reassure her that what they were doing was truly the best thing for everyone concerned, but he didn't know for certain that it was. Their plan was unusual at best and plain old foolish at worst.

Sure, he had his own concerns, but he wasn't about to share those with Charli. She didn't need to know how he was struggling with his emotions, which were sometimes so strong he could barely keep them inside.

Talk about complicating things. They had enough to worry about with the ranch and Levi's guardianship. He didn't need to add how confused he felt about her to the mix, at least not right now.

The best thing he could do was continue to support her in every way he knew how and pray that true love would eventually find a path to their door.

Chapter Ten

"We have a court date," Charli announced as she entered Henry's cabin a few mornings later. "It's three weeks from Tuesday."

"Three *weeks*?" Henry echoed, raising his eyebrows. He was mid diaper change with a wiggly baby boy, so he kept his attention on Levi even as it appeared fireworks were going off behind his eyes. "So soon? For some reason I thought it would be longer before we actually got a date in court."

"I know. I assumed the exact same thing. Do you think it could possibly be this easy? I thought it would be a slow uphill battle, but now I feel as if we're sliding down an icy embankment and are picking up speed as we go."

Henry chuckled as he finished snapping up the red one-piece Levi was wearing and picked up the baby, placing him on his broad shoulder. "I feel the same way. Although your analogy leaves something to be desired. I'd rather not be caught in an avalanche."

Charli knew her realist attitude didn't always strike Henry right, and she joined him with her laughter.

"Knock, knock," came a high, cheerful voice at the same time as literal knocking on the front door.

Charli took a deep breath. It was Fiona, here for her

first time babysitting Levi while Charli and Henry spent the day mending fences in the far fields. They had some serious work to do before winter hit, and fencing was much easier as a two-person job, setting new poles and wrapping the barbed wire that would keep the cattle safe. And while Charli was still iffy about leaving the baby with anyone, she was beginning to slowly trust Fiona and was relieved she'd be the babysitter for their first time leaving Levi.

Did all parents feel this way? Or was she just being extra cautious because of all Levi had already been through in his young life?

"Hey, Fiona," Henry said as he opened the door to his cabin. "Thanks for offering to watch the baby today. We really appreciate your help."

"Absolutely my pleasure," she said, cooing nonsensically to Levi as she reached out for him. "We are going to have so much fun today, aren't we?" She smothered the baby's chubby cheek with kisses and then turned her attention to Charli. "So what are you two up to today? Anything romantic? I think they ought to share their secrets with Auntie Fiona, don't you, Levi?" she murmured into the baby's ear.

Charli snorted with laughter, then smothered her smile. If only Fiona knew just how much she and Henry were entirely missing romance in their relationship. That was actually the big secret. "Nothing romantic, unless you count repairing fences."

"Wood posts. Barbed wire," Henry added. "A regular recipe for love."

Love?

Charli's gaze flashed to Henry's, but he steadfastly

refused to look at her, though his cheeks reddened. Evidently even the word *love* unsettled him, just as it did her.

She was a long way off from even considering romance—like, on their wedding day far off. Only then would she give herself leave to consider what the rest of their lives would look like.

"Okay, so mending fences doesn't sound like much fun," Fiona agreed. "Not any more than if you're doing it metaphorically instead of literally. But I suppose actually mending fences is part and parcel of owning a ranch."

Charli's heart jumped as Henry finally lifted his gaze to meet hers—presumably because Fiona was speaking as if keeping the ranch was a matter of course.

And that was all it should be within their business arrangement. Yet there was a little something more, something in the warm twinkle of Henry's eyes that Charli didn't quite know what to do with. If she was being honest with herself, and it was about time she started doing that, she was looking forward to spending the day with Henry, even if it was simply doing ranch work. It was no different than any of the other multitude of times they'd spent all day repairing fences or herding cattle, and yet, there it was. That indefinable...

Something.

A thrill of that *something* she absolutely refused to name skittered up Charli's spine.

As Henry reviewed baby care instructions with Fiona, Charli swallowed hard and forcefully yanked herself out of her confused thoughts and emotions.

"I'll have my cell phone on me," Charli told Fiona. "Feel free to call me about anything. Anything at all. No question or concern is too small."

"Don't worry. I will. But Levi and I are going to do great together." She pressed her cheek to Levi's and waved his arm at them. "Bye-bye, Daddy and Mama. Have a great day, and don't forget to have some fun along the way."

"We will," Henry assured her with a dippy grin, and Charli wanted to roll her eyes even as her heart turned over. She was going to have to talk to Henry about encouraging Fiona in her romanticized ideas of what living on a ranch was all about. They already had cattle with *names*. If they didn't tamp down Fiona's bubbly outlook on the world, who knew what would be next?

Purchasing geese or a mule just because they were *cute* and not in any way useful to their ranch? She could see her sister petitioning for something like that. And somehow, she thought Henry might give in. He was a strong, sturdy rancher, yes, but he was also hiding a soft heart underneath that gruff exterior.

They took Henry's truck to the fence line, since it was the easiest way to tote the materials they'd need to make the repairs. He parked next to their first destination of the day, a section of torn up fencing that needed to be completely replaced. It looked as if a vehicle had driven through it, so it was a major repair.

With the ease of years of ranch work performed together, Henry pulled on his thick leather work gloves, jammed wire cutters into the back pocket of his jeans, grabbed a hole digger from the back of the truck and set to work removing the damaged poles and replacing them with new ones.

Charli helped whenever he needed a hand, but she found herself more than a little distracted by Henry, everything from his biceps straining against his long-sleeved blue Henley to the wire cutters dangling from the back pocket of his worn blue jeans. How had she never before noticed his scent, a subtle mix of aged leather, crisp evergreen and unique male, something distinctly Henry that made her head swim?

She was turning into a regular goose where Henry was concerned. She needed to watch herself or she'd become seriously lost in her daydreams.

"Charli?" Henry's voice intruded on her thoughts.

"Hmm?"

"I asked how you think our court appearance is going to go."

And she hadn't even heard him because she'd been woolgathering.

About *him*.

Her cheeks heated. "I suppose a lot of it depends on what kind of judge we have," Charli said thoughtfully. "I hope we get someone nice and kind who will understand our predicament and rule in our favor. Otherwise, I don't know what we'll do. Appeal, I suppose, though I really hope it doesn't come to that. You're Levi's only living relative who is willing to step up and pledge to be his guardian, especially since your folks won't do it. What more could they ask for? I think we need to continue to think positive here."

Not that *thinking positive* was really her thing. Praying for the best outcome, however—that she could do.

"Three weeks, though. That doesn't seem like nearly enough time for us to get our case together."

"Why not?" she challenged him. "We've prepared as much as we can, haven't we?"

"Are you sure we shouldn't hire a lawyer who will put our case front and center?" He sounded iffy. "I know

Amber Goodwin is helping us out of the kindness of her heart, but it's pro bono work because she feels sorry for our situation. I'm not sure how much time she really has to put into our case, and I worry it won't be enough."

Charli had grown up with Amber who worked in family law, so Charli had immediately thought of her.

"We talked about this. You and I are both cash poor at the moment, and honestly, I'm not sure what difference paying a lawyer would make. Amber knows us and our situation. There isn't really much else we can do now besides show up and present you as the best option to be Levi's guardian. Amber said she believed there was no reason a judge would decide to rule against us once they've read the letter your sister left you. Also, Amber promised to be there on the day of our court appearance to represent us, and you'll be there to step up to the stand and speak for yourself if you have to, to let the judge know you understand the responsibility you're taking on in accepting legal guardianship of the baby with the final goal of adopting Levi as your own son."

"I agree with you. But three weeks? That doesn't seem very long to me. It makes me nervous."

"We can do it."

"I'm not talking about court right now. What I mean is, what are we going to do about our wedding?" Henry scratched at the dark scruff on his cheek. "We haven't really talked about *when* we planned to get married. I guess I didn't realize how important it was to get right on it. I thought we'd have more time. And now we're suddenly in a crunch. What do you think? Should we elope before then?"

Elope?

Charli was already feeling rushed by the whole idea

of marriage, and the reality of them tying the knot within the next three weeks was as overwhelming as a Montana blizzard whiteout, making it impossible for her to see or breathe. A frisson of ice walked down her spine, and she shivered. Henry sounded perfectly serious about his suggestion, as if they could just hop on their horses and ride off into the sunset together—at least until the evening ranch chores were due.

"Do you really think we have to be married?" she asked hesitantly. "Before the court date, I mean?"

His eyes narrowed on her, worry lines creasing his forehead. He lifted his black cowboy hat and dabbed at his forehead with the back of his hand. "As opposed to what? I thought the whole point of us getting hitched was so the court would see us together as a couple for Levi's sake. So we can both become his legal guardians and eventually his parents."

"It is. And we will—raise Levi together as partners, I mean. I promised you I'd be Levi's mama, and I will be. I just don't see any way we can legitimately make the wedding happen so fast. Like you said, we haven't really talked about the logistics, but I don't want to get married at a courthouse in front of a justice of the peace or race off to Las Vegas and have an Elvis impersonator officiating. Our engagement hasn't been in any way traditional, but it's important to me that we say our vows in church before God and, as much as I hate to admit it, in front of my family. I want to walk down the aisle to you."

He smiled softly. "I totally agree. I'll be standing at the front of the church waiting for you to make our vows together. I wouldn't have it any other way. Even though this isn't exactly a typical situation for either of us, I want you to have the wedding of your dreams."

"Then it can't be done. Not in the current time frame. And not because I'm holding on to some silly white dress, bouquets of flowers, big cake wedding nonsense from my childhood." Charli shook her head definitively. "I'm not that type of woman and never have been. But even so, that doesn't help us much. There are other considerations, so we'll have to come up with another plan for how we're going to handle the court date. Hopefully it will be enough that we're engaged, because there is no way we're going to be getting married within the next three weeks."

"Why not?" Henry used every bit of his strength to wiggle a worn post loose and then kicked it with his cowboy boot, knocking it out of the way before jamming the hole digger into the open spot. Charli could tell his feelings were involved in this conversation. She almost felt sorry for the poor fence post.

She sighed. "There are many reasons this isn't going to work."

Henry jolted up as if a lightning bolt had hit him and Charli quickly held up a hand. "In the short term, I mean. I doubt our pastor is going to marry us without premarital counseling, for starters."

"Really? Isn't that optional?"

"I'm not a hundred percent certain without speaking to Pastor Thomas first, but I don't think so. Some of my friends have gotten married in the church, and I remember them telling me the Pre-Cana course was an absolute requirement and took something like six months to complete."

"Six *months*?" Henry shook his head. "I had no idea it would take that long. I guess I figured from the beginning that this would be more of a shotgun wedding—minus the shotgun. If your sisters agree to your terms, it will probably be worthwhile for us to lock up the ranch ownership as soon as possible. And like you said—you want your family there for the wedding."

"Good point. I've been so busy between my mom and sisters, the baby and the ranch that I haven't even had time to look at my calendar or talk to Pastor Thomas about our upcoming nuptials. Maybe if we pick our wedding date he could be persuaded to meet with us for counseling after we've tied the knot, as long as we can convince him we completely understand what we're getting into," Charli said.

"You mean like *until death do us part*?"

"Exactly."

"I don't need counseling to understand that part, and to be honest, I don't know why I need to prove myself to anyone other than you. Why do we need to go to premarital counseling at all? You know me better than anyone, which is why you came to me when you experienced trouble with your family. As you well know, I only intend to do this once. If you marry me, you already understand going into it that divorce isn't even on the table for us. My parents got divorced. So did yours. We've seen it in action. I'm not going to do that to you, or to Levi." Henry clipped off stray wire with the cutters as if putting punctuation on the end of his statement.

"My thoughts exactly. As a matter of fact, I suggest it ought to be a rule going into our marriage. No threatening divorce even in anger. We shouldn't use that word against each other. Ever."

"I agree." He shoved the pole digger into the ground with a grunt of exertion, and maybe emotion, as well.

"So, in six weeks, maybe? I'll talk to the pastor and

see if he and the church are available, and we can nail this down. Then we'll have an exact date to provide to the court so we can prove we're serious."

"As soon as we get the go-ahead, we'll tell your family." He stopped and leaned his forearm on the pole digger, making his shoulders ripple under his Henley. Charli was momentarily sidetracked by that movement, and she mentally chastised herself. She was starting to lose it on a regular basis. She'd worked with Henry since they'd been teenagers. And now that they were getting married for what amounted to business reasons, she suddenly noticed him as a man?

What was wrong with her?

"Charli?" he asked, and her gaze moved up to his eyes. Clearly, he'd asked her a question and once again, she'd missed it.

"I'm sorry. I was just thinking about all we have to get done in the next few weeks." She hadn't been, but she wasn't about to tell Henry she'd been thinking about *him*. "Did you ask me a question?"

Henry made a sound from deep in his throat and nodded. "Yeah. I wondered if you want me to talk to your mom first. You know, ask her for her blessing on our marriage?"

"Ha!" Charli burst out before she could stop herself. "Absolutely not."

"Okay. I just thought—"

She shook her head. "No. It's not you. Look, I know you're an honorable man," she interrupted before he could go and make any kind of declaration that would majorly complicate both of their lives. "And despite our beginning, you want to do this the right way. But our marriage is between you and me. We don't need her blessing, and frankly,

I don't want to give her the opportunity to tear us down in any way. I don't need that right now, and neither do you."

Out of nowhere, Charli suddenly felt as if a stampede of cattle had run over her as her heart filled with almost unbearable heaviness. Grief was like that. She never knew when it would sneak up on her and grab her around the neck from behind, and this was one of those times.

Feeling as if her trembling legs would no longer hold her, she staggered over to Henry's truck and hopped onto the tailgate, burying her face in her hands. Even that small movement had her struggling for air, and she gasped for a breath.

Henry was by her side in a second. "Charli? Sweetheart? Are you okay? Did I say something wrong?"

Gripping the emotions swirling through her, Charli waited for the tears to come, but despite the whiteout of the blizzard raging through her, her eyes remained dry.

Henry tipped her chin up so he could meet her gaze. "What's going on?" he asked gently. "I can tell you're struggling."

"If Daddy were here," she said, her voice trembling, "everything would be different. I would have wanted you to seek his blessing. He was so proud of you, you know, how you pulled yourself up by your bootstraps and made something of yourself. I know he would have given us his blessing with all his heart."

Henry's face reddened at her praise, and he reached out and grabbed hold of both of Charli's hands. "I had so much respect for that man."

"You must know how much Daddy loved you. He considered you the son he never had. I think he's looking down from heaven with a smile on his face at the thought that you'll officially be part of the family. Somehow, I believe he would have wanted this."

"I—" Henry started, then had to stop and clear his throat from the gruffness suddenly there. "I think so, too. Maybe things are working out the way they're supposed to."

"Do you think?"

Henry nodded thoughtfully. "Seems to me God has left our way forward wide open. I help you, you help me. I don't believe in coincidences. I believe in God things."

God things. That was exactly how Henry viewed life. Charli wished she had the same kind of black and white faith. She saw only shades of gray, especially now.

"I may be the strangest female ever, but I never dreamed about having a huge wedding as a little girl. I didn't think about what kind of dress I wanted, or what flavor of cake or kind of flowers. My dreams always involved horses and ranches, and I'd probably be happy and more comfortable getting married in blue jeans and cowboy boots. But there was one thing—I always imagined my father walking me down the aisle if I ever did get married. And now he's the one thing missing from this scenario."

Henry squeezed her hands. "Not missing. It's just different. He's still here watching over you. I know you can feel him here."

"Yeah." She sighed. "I can."

He paused, then spoke again. "Speaking of wedding stuff. Are you planning to do any of that? Your mom and sisters are probably going to expect some show of excitement on our part or else they'll get suspicious."

"Ugh," Charli said with a groan. "Only because they don't know me. If they did, they'd know better. But yes.

You're right. I'm going to have to expend some effort to make this wedding happen. Fiona is practically bouncing off the walls as it is, pushing me to go wedding dress shopping. Even my mom has mentioned it a couple of times. Who knew they'd consider it a familial bonding experience? It sounds like torture to me. My plan at this point is to find a dress off the rack, and you can just wear that navy blue suit you wear on Christmas and Easter. Or if you're really getting into the spirit of things, you could always rent a tux," she teased.

Henry jerked a nod, but Charli had the oddest impression something was bothering him.

"Henry?" she asked. He turned away, but not before she caught a flash of something in his expressive blue eyes. She was good at reading him, and his emotions at this point were blaring silent sirens at her.

Pain? But why?

After an afternoon of repairing fences, Henry pulled up to the front of his cabin. A silent Charli was seated next to him. She'd been lost in thought and hardly said a word after they'd talked about the wedding. Not that he could blame her. He was feeling overwhelmed as well.

A *tuxedo*? Ugh. His throat was closing at the mere thought of a bow tie.

"I'll be inside in just a minute," Henry said, hanging back as they got out of the truck. He could tell how hard grief was hitting Charli, even though she'd remained dry-eyed and stoic. Of course she would have wanted John to walk her down the aisle.

She was strong and resilient, his Charli. His *fiancée*. He admired her so much. And he wanted to pinch himself every time he thought about the fact that she'd chosen him as her life partner.

What could he do to show his support? He wasn't good with emotions and especially not with words. So what did a man do to show appreciation for his future wife?

He glanced around, and after a minute or so came up with a solution. Not a perfect plan by any means, but hopefully something to raise her spirits, to let her know he was thinking of her as a man regarded the woman to whom he'd committed his life.

And devoted his heart, though she didn't know that.

His gaze wandered over the wonder of the colors of the Montana mountains, the beautiful land for which she was fighting so hard. Creating a bouquet of wildflowers wasn't exactly part of Henry's natural skillsets and it hadn't worked out that well when he'd picked her a bloom last time, but maybe this time would be different. He selected a range of colors and sizes and carefully bundled them up in his fist.

Feeling he'd done the best he could, he hid the clutch of wildflowers behind his back and strode inside the cabin, eager to relieve Fiona of her babysitting duties and spend some quality time with his nephew.

"There you are, Henry!" Charli's sister exclaimed in her usually bubbly voice. Henry laughed and shook his head, his gaze meeting Charli's. She rolled her eyes, clearly not enamored of her copper-haired sister's bright enthusiasm.

Not for the first time, he wondered how three sisters could be so different from each other, not only in looks but especially in personality. Charli hadn't grown up with Fiona and Cordelia, but even so. Their dispositions were as different as could be.

With both women's gazes on him, he couldn't have been more nervous if he'd been the center of attention in a huge room full of people. He cleared his throat and turned to Charli, tipping his hat. "I, er, picked these for you," he stammered, revealing his makeshift bouquet and stretching it out toward her with a grin that felt much more like a grimace.

Her gaze widened and her jaw dropped, but she didn't immediately reach for the odd combination of flowers. He continued to hold them out to her, feeling increasingly awkward with every moment that passed.

Why wasn't she taking the flowers?

Fiona squealed and stepped forward, pushing her sister toward the colorful bunch until Charli had no choice but to grab them or else get a face full of wildflowers. Even after she'd taken the flowers, she didn't appear to know what to do with them. She looked up at him and met his gaze, but her eyes were glassy, and he couldn't tell what she was thinking.

He had the distinct impression he'd just made a grave error. But why?

Yes, their relationship was changing, but that was the point of his gesture, to show he acknowledged the newness between them.

"These are absolutely lovely," Fiona said, and Henry wondered why she was speaking instead of Charli. Fiona shifted the baby into his arms and took the bouquet meant for Charli. "All these lovely colors. I'll just put these in water," she said, dismissing herself from their presence.

"Charli?" Henry asked as soon as Fiona had left the room. "What—"

"Flowers, Henry?" Charli asked.

Was she angry he'd brought in a makeshift bouquet? Why would she be mad? Because he'd picked them instead of buying them? He'd never claimed to understand women, but this was a new low even for him. He was beyond confused. He obviously wasn't fiancé material. Up until the time they'd become engaged, their relationship had been well defined, even if he had harbored long-term unreciprocated feelings for her. As long as he'd kept them well-hidden, there hadn't been any problems.

"What did I do wrong?" he asked Charli in a low voice, just in case Fiona was still within earshot. Maybe if he understood what she was feeling, he wouldn't repeat his mistake in the future.

"I'm not..." she started, then paused, running a hand down her face with a sigh. "Never mind. I see what you're trying to do here, and it's probably a good idea. Fiona can't keep anything to herself, so my entire family will know about the flowers by tonight."

Henry's heart squeezed so tightly he thought it might burst. She hadn't understood what he was trying to do at all. "I—" he began, then stopped. How had she not gotten that the flowers were for *her* and not as some kind of fake display for Fiona's sake? "I tried to pick the blooms I know you like," he pointed out. "All your favorites."

She smiled softly. "I noticed."

So she *had* noticed what he'd done for her. At least to some degree.

Now Henry's heart was squeezing for an entirely different reason. What her smile did to him was almost beyond bearing. He suddenly felt like a goofy teenager on his first date. Not that he'd dated a lot as a teenager. He'd been gangly and gawky, all arms and legs, and as if that wasn't enough, had been relegated to special education classes in school because of his struggles with dyslexia and dysgraphia. Was it any wonder that he'd dropped out of school without graduating?

"Here we go," Fiona said, returning to the living room with a vase of carefully arranged blooms. "Do you want to keep them here or take them to the big house?"

Charli shrugged, looking dazed.

"How about the mantel over the fireplace?" Henry suggested.

"Perfect," Fiona agreed before turning back to Charli. "Speaking of flowers... Have you considered what kind of flowers you're going to use for your wedding? Something traditional, or are you thinking more contemporary?"

Charli frowned and her face blanched to an alarming white that would probably match her as-yet-unbought wedding dress. "Oh, I don't think flowers are really going to be necessary," she protested. "We're getting married in about a month, so the less complicated we make things, the better."

"Of course you need flowers," Fiona objected, and Henry privately agreed with her. Yes, they needed to tie the knot sooner rather than later, but he still wanted Charli to have the wedding of her dreams—if he could figure out what that was.

"And we need to go dress shopping," Fiona continued. "Mama, Cordelia and I will all accompany you. We'll make a day of it. Cake shopping. Flower shopping. Do you have any plans for a reception venue yet?"

Henry didn't miss the way Charli's shoulders tensed. Her face had gone from white to red and she looked about ready to explode like an active volcano, but Fiona didn't appear to notice. "Maybe we can go sometime this week. I'll talk to Mama and Cordelia and get back to you on it, okay?"

"Sounds good," Charli croaked, and Henry knew just how much effort it took her to agree to what she clearly considered pure torment.

The moment Fiona gathered her things and left the cabin, Charli whirled on him. "This is all your fault," she accused, her hands perched on her hips and her gaze narrowing on him. "Dress shopping? Really?"

While his heart hurt for her, knowing how uncomfortable she was, he tried to hide his smile but couldn't. She was just too cute when she was squirming. "Well, you do need a wedding dress, right? As much as you may want to, you can't get married in jeans and cowboy boots in church. We dress better than that on Sundays. And maybe spending some quality time with your mom and sisters will give you the opportunity to work things out with them."

"Why do I still feel as if I'm sliding down a steep, icy hill?" she said.

He nodded in agreement. "Because you are. We are. No doubt about it. But we have to focus on what's at the bottom of the hill."

"And that would that be what? A crash landing?"

He grinned. "A ranch with our name on it."

"Point taken. But if I have to try on wedding dresses, you have to go pick out a tux."

"What? No. Why would I need to do that? I have my Sunday suit."

"Not good enough," she insisted, though he was certain it was more to make him squirm as he'd just done to her than because she had anything against his Sunday best. "It's only fair, and you get the easy way out. You won't even have to spend the day with family the way I do."

"Are you serious? I don't know how to pick out a tux." There. That should be the end of the conversation.

"Of course you don't. That's why you go to a tux rental shop where they have experts to help you. I wish my own father could be here to go with you, but you can take Mason along. I'm sure he wouldn't mind."

Mason Campbell had been John Stafford's best friend and was Charli's beloved godfather. Henry's own family had pretty much disowned him when he'd dropped out of high school, and he'd floundered until John had given him a job on his ranch and the opportunity to make something of himself. And Mason had always treated Henry with respect. Charli was right. Mason would work in a pinch.

"I'll call and ask him," Charli pressed.

Henry reluctantly nodded his assent. As much as visiting a tux rental shop sounded right up there with getting dental work done, he owed it to Charli, since she was going to be equally suffering when trying on wedding dresses, and with her family, no less.

Quid pro quo, he supposed.

Only it wouldn't be, because any amount of discomfort on his part was worth getting to see Charli walk down the aisle to him in her wedding dress. Could he help it if he was looking forward to that moment with all his heart?

Chapter Eleven

Charli reluctantly entered the dress shop led by her solemn mother and followed by her chitter-chattering sisters, determined to create a party out of this day. She swallowed hard as she looked about her, nearly overwhelmed by the white and lace and frills everywhere and feeling decidedly less cheery than her family. How had she managed to let them talk her into this situation?

A saleswoman appeared from the back room with a measuring tape draped around her neck. "Who's the bride-to-be?" she asked jovially.

Charli cringed inwardly as she waved a finger. "That would be me."

"And you all must be her sisters," the saleswoman said with a knowing grin.

"Nice try," Martha said with a look of derision, though Charli noticed her cheeks warmed at the compliment. "Mother of the bride."

Now it was Charli's turn to blush. This whole thing just seemed wrong in so many ways. Martha had never been a mother to her, at least not that she remembered. But now it was important that they present a united front.

For the sake of the ranch, she reminded herself.

This, though, trying on wedding dresses, was so far

beyond Charli's comfort zone that it wasn't even funny. She only wore loose, casual maxi dresses to church. Wedding dresses were way too formal for her taste.

"Do you have an idea in mind for what type of dress you're looking for? Traditional? Mermaid cut? Sheer overlay? Ruffles? Satin? And what about sleeves? Cap? Off the shoulder? And the neckline? Sweetheart? V-neck? Scoop? Square?"

Charli had never passed out in her life, not even when she'd been thrown headfirst off a horse she was gentling, but right now she felt dizzy enough to faint outright. She headed for the nearest chair to slump in.

To her surprise, Martha was right at her side, gently patting her shoulder. "It's a lot, I know," she whispered for Charli's ears alone—easily done, since Fiona and Cordelia were already excitedly checking out the racks of dresses. "Don't let it overwhelm you. Just try to breathe through it. We'll find you something that represents *you*, okay?"

"I...thank you," said Charli, swallowing hard through a dry throat.

"Can we get a design book over here, please?" Martha asked the saleswoman. "I'd like for Charli to be able to look at a few designs before checking the racks."

"Certainly. That's a wonderful place to start. Let me know if you'd like to see a certain cut," the saleswoman said.

"Oh, Charli. Look at this one," Fiona said, holding a skintight mermaid cut gown in front of her. "Isn't this lovely?"

Charli cringed. Lovely for Fiona, absolutely. She had the figure and the personality for it. But Charli knew she wouldn't be able to walk in that dress, and she'd look ridiculous trying. She pictured herself scooting her feet along like a geisha with the material bound tightly around her legs.

"No. Just no," Charli said adamantly, then tried to backpedal, afraid she may have accidentally hurt Fiona's feelings. "I can't see myself in that dress. It would look super cute on you, though."

"I'll have to keep it in mind for when it's my turn to walk down the aisle," Fiona agreed pleasantly, apparently not taken aback by Charli's lack of enthusiasm.

"Not so much for me," Cordelia said. "I'm so over it."

Charli remembered Cordelia mentioned something about not having anything to go back to in Denver and wondered if that had something to do with it.

"Cordelia's just coming off a bad breakup," Fiona explained. "The guy was a real jerk to her. Personally, I think she's better off without him."

Cordelia snorted. "I'm standing right here," she reminded her sister. "I can hear you, you know."

"I'm sorry that happened to you, Cordelia," Charli said, and meant it. "I'm sure he wasn't good enough for you."

Seeing how hurt Cordelia clearly was by her breakup, Charli found herself grateful that she'd been too busy running the ranch to have had anything other than the most casual of dating relationships, and nothing that had been serious enough to break her heart.

Now she was marrying Henry, a man who made her feel safe. Protected. Warm inside.

And...*special*.

It may not be the most customary of marriages, but the closer they got to the day of the wedding, the more certain she was that she was making the right choice in marrying this man and tying her life to him.

Her choice of a dress, not so much. How could it be that picking a man was easier than picking out clothing? And yet, here she was...

Taking a deep breath, she dove into the fashion book, flipping page after page, trying and failing to imagine herself in any of the designs. She quickly nixed plunging necklines and skintight cuts of any nature as not being her style. If she had to wear a wedding dress, she would go with something more traditional.

Even if she did look like a goof in lace and frills.

After a few minutes of browsing the book, she and her sisters moved to the rack labeled for traditional dresses and started perusing the choices—at least until Charli took a gander at the price tags. Suddenly it was all she could do to breathe without choking.

Were they *serious*? How could a dress she was only going to wear once in her life for a few mere hours cost hundreds of dollars, some into four figures? Clearly she'd been living in country oblivion not to have known this.

"What's wrong?" her mom asked when Charli dropped her hands to her sides and stepped away from the rack, heat rising to her face as she swallowed hard. "Still having problems finding something you think is suitable?"

"Have you seen the prices on these things?" she hissed under her breath. "It's highway robbery."

"Of course it is," Martha said practically. "They bargain that you're only going to get married once, so they can hook you however they want to. You can't argue with that."

"Oh, I *so* can. That's a big *nope* from me."

"Because of the price tag? Don't worry about it. It's on me. As a wedding gift to you. It's the least I can do, as much trouble as I've given you and Henry."

"Mom," Charli objected, though Fiona and Cordelia didn't appear to find anything wrong with their mom offering to pay for a ridiculously priced dress. Charli's heart was bouncing all over her chest—partly in surprise, partly in gratitude that her mother seemed to care so much, and partly in confusion for the very same reasons. As far as she knew, Martha was still staunchly in favor of selling the ranch.

Or had something changed she didn't know about? She sounded as if she was changing her mind about Henry. That was something, at least.

Still, she couldn't let her mom throw her money away.

"That's very generous, but I can't let you do that," Charli protested.

"You can and you will," her mom argued. Did everyone have as much trouble as Charli did standing up to her own mother? What was it about the relationship that made it so hard not to listen to whatever Mom was saying?

"Do you have a clearance rack?" Charli asked the saleswoman, who raised her eyebrows and quirked her lips before answering.

"We do have one rack—I hesitate to call it *clearance*—where you can buy the dress directly off the hanger without alterations, though I personally don't recommend it."

Unlike how difficult it was for Charli to ignore her mother's wishes, she frankly couldn't care less about the saleswoman's opinions and made a beeline to the rack in question, quickly thumbing through the dresses one by one, rejecting first one and then the next.

"No. Nope. Absolutely not." Charli wasn't having any more success finding a dress here than she had elsewhere in the shop.

Fiona reached out and grasped Charli's hands in hers, turning her to face her so their eyes met. "Deep breath in," her sister said, encouraging her. "Hold it for five seconds. Now, deep breath out."

Charli did as she was told. It helped. A little.

"I think what you need to do is actually try on a dress," Fiona suggested with a soft smile. "Even if it's totally the wrong one, it'll get your brain going in the right direction. What do you think?"

Charli sighed, loud and dramatic. "I think I'm wasting my time."

"Trust me," Fiona said. "It'll make a difference."

"Fine," Charli finally agreed, more to have her sister get off her back than anything else.

"Now…which dress will you choose first?" Fiona urged.

After refusing to even consider the majority of the racks of dresses—either because they were ridiculously high priced or were cut in ways that made Charli want to roll her eyes—or both—her sisters finally convinced her to try on a traditional dress with lace and a train off the *Sold-As-Is* rack.

Her entire family herded her into a dressing room and insisted she close her eyes once she'd donned the dress so they could lead her out to a three-way mirror and arrange it around her. She felt ridiculous.

Why was she having a giddy feeling in her stomach about something that meant nothing to her?

She was doing this for other people, not for herself.

She wondered if Henry was feeling the same way, as if their whole wedding had been taken out of their hands and other people were running away with it. She was fairly certain Henry didn't care whether they got married in a tux and white dress or jeans and cowboy boots, except out of respect for the church...and now to please her family.

When had all this become so complicated?

"Okay...open your eyes," Fiona announced, punctuating her sentence with a squeal of delight.

Charli tried not to sigh as she opened her eyes, expecting to look ridiculous in a frilly getup, but when she saw herself, her jaw dropped until she was gaping at her reflection in the mirror.

Who was this woman looking back at her?

The gown accentuated her figure without being clingy. The lace and pearls were tasteful without overwhelming the dress. And the train made her feel as if she were a...

Princess.

"Here," Martha said, stepping forward with a sparkling tiara and carefully placing it on Charli's head. "What do you think? Unless you want a veil instead?"

"No. I—I," Charli stammered, unable to voice her thoughts.

Instead of feeling boxed up and awkward in this garb, she felt, for the first time since she'd proposed to Henry... like a bride.

Henry's gaze widened as he stepped into the tuxedo rental shop. Prior to today, he'd had no idea so many colors of suits and tuxes even existed, solids and patterns of all varieties, and that was to say nothing of the different kinds of vests, cummerbunds, ties and other claptrap to go along with them. He supposed he'd been expecting only classic black and hadn't given any thought at all to anything else.

He was glad Mason had come with him, someone older and wiser, able to handle this kind of thing. Though Mason had never married, he'd still been willing to step in for John and act as a father figure to have Henry's back in this oh-so-important moment. Henry wished his own father was interested in his life, but that ship had sailed a long time ago. They'd never forgiven him for dropping out of high school and weren't even on a speaking basis with him—or each other, for that matter. It broke his heart, but there was nothing he could do about it. He'd tried to call them to inform them of his upcoming marriage with a last-ditch hope that one or both would consider coming to his wedding, but neither his mom nor dad would even answer their cell phones. They'd probably blocked him.

"Wow. Lots of colors to choose from," Mason said, with a low whistle, brushing his overlong white hair out of his eyes with a quick flick of his chin. "Did Charli or Martha give you any clue as to which direction you ought to be going here?"

Henry tried to say no, but the word came out as a barely audible squeak, like he'd sounded going through puberty in adolescence. He cleared his throat and tried again in a lower register. "No. If I'd have known there were so many choices, I would have asked for some guidance."

"That's part of the reason I came out with you today," Mason said. "Not so much to give you guidance on your suit, but to talk to you about Charli."

Mason's lips turned down into a frown, and Henry swallowed hard. "What about Charli?"

"I want to make sure you understand what you're getting into," Mason said. "You're making a lifetime commitment to my goddaughter, and I'm going to hold you to that. You hurt her, you answer to me. That's what John would have wanted."

Henry nodded. "Yes, sir. You have my word that I'll take care of her, cherish her and protect her."

Mason cocked his head to one side, his gaze narrowing. "And will you love her the way she deserves to be loved?"

Henry's chest filled with longing, but as much as he wanted to, he couldn't say the words Mason wanted to hear. If and when he declared those words, they would first be said to Charli. He stiffened and broke his gaze away from the older man's.

Mason's frown deepened. "Henry? Why aren't you answering me? Are you not prepared to make the kind of commitment my goddaughter deserves?"

"I would never do her wrong," Henry said, his voice like gravel. "I mean, yes, my commitment to Charli is wholehearted."

Mason continued frowning at him for a moment more, and then suddenly he grinned. "See that it stays that way."

The salesman was eyeing them and hovering close by, clearly sizing them up for a sale, so Henry, happy to be out of a whole new kind of godfather territory, brought the topic back around to his tuxedo. "Any ideas on what I should choose for a suit?"

"Hang on," Mason said. "Let me call Charli and see what she says."

Henry wandered around the store while Mason spoke to Charli. Seeing all the choices got him all wound up like a panther about to pounce upon his prey. Every nerve in his body felt as if it were on a spring. Talk about overwhelming.

He had to remind himself of why he was doing this before he obeyed the screaming voice in the back of his head and bolted.

So Levi's guardianship would go through without a hitch.

And for Charli's ranch, so she could keep her beloved land, and their new little family would have a permanent place to live. Yes, deep down, he wanted to co-own the ranch with her. That much was true.

But most of all, this was for Charli. To make her happy.

This was really happening.

Of course, he'd *known* the wedding was happening. But picturing himself in a tuxedo waiting at the altar for Charli so they could tie their lives together in holy matrimony?

What was he doing?

What if someday Charli had regrets about their marriage, about not being in love with the person to whom she'd tied herself for life?

Was he just being a hopeless romantic? This was real life.

"Okay, got it," said Mason, pocketing his cell phone as he approached. "I think I have all the info we need. We caught them at a good time."

"Them?" He'd thought Mason was texting Charli.

"The ladies, including Martha, are all out wedding dress shopping today."

Henry nodded. He'd known that, although his mind had completely blanked out the fact the moment he'd walked in this store.

"So anyway, I got everyone's opinion on the matter—some louder than others, if you know what I mean." He clicked his tongue.

Henry cringed inwardly, imagining what that must have been like for Charli. She was probably feeling just as overwhelmed as he was, even more so because she was shopping with her entire estranged family. Her sisters and mom probably had a lot to say, far more opinions than Charli would seek, and she wasn't keen on dress shopping to begin with. He imagined Martha and Charli's sisters like a henhouse, with everyone clucking out what they thought Charli should wear. He sent up a short, silent prayer for her patience.

At least Mason was easy to get along with. And Henry was actually hoping Mason would have opinions to share, because he was totally lost on this.

"I, uh, really only care what Charli thinks," he admitted.

"I figured." Mason choked out a low, scratchy laugh. His eyes gleamed with amusement in the bright fluorescent lighting. With anyone else, Henry would have felt uncomfortable, as if they might be laughing at him and not with him. That had happened enough times in his life, from the time he was a small child until adulthood.

But with Mason, not so much. Mason treated him with respect.

"So—what, then?" Henry asked, curious as to Charli's opinions.

"Charli wants her wedding colors to be scarlet and lime green, so maybe some kind of combination of the two colors? She specifically requested lots of ruffles—down the front and at your wrists."

Henry felt his face blanch and knew he must look as white as a sheet. Mason was able to hold a straight face for all of five seconds before he burst out in laughter so loud it brought a second sales attendant forward from the back room.

Mason laughed so hard he had tears in his eyes. He wiped them away with the back of one hand and pointed at Henry with the other. "You should have seen your face."

"Scarlet and lime green? Really? You had me scared there for a second."

"You know the worst part in all this? You would have actually worn those colors if I'd been serious—I mean, if that was what she'd really said."

Henry shrugged, refusing to acknowledge Mason's question. The scary thing was, he probably would have. There wasn't much he wouldn't do for Charli, up to and including wearing nausea-inducing colors.

"It's saying a lot about how you feel about her that you're even willing to get gussied up in a tux at all," Mason said.

"We both want a church wedding, and her family was adamant about her wearing a white dress. I don't think she really cares much one way or the other."

"Naw. Not really Charli's personality, is it?"

Henry shook his head. "It isn't about the wedding. It's about the marriage. So, what did she say that wasn't scarlet and lime green? Any real direction for us?"

"At first, she said she thought traditional black would be best, but then everyone started talking in the background about selecting something royal blue. Because it'll bring out the *gorgeous blue in your eyes*," Mason teased in a high, nasal tone, framing his trim white beard with his palms and blinking his eyelashes rapidly.

"Cut it out," Henry barked back, feeling his own cheeks flame.

"Just repeating what they said."

"So, I guess I'll go with blue, then." He turned to the sales associate. "A tuxedo in blue, please. Uh, for me."

"*Royal* blue," Mason added helpfully. "I guess there are several shades of blue to choose from."

Henry's gaze widened. "There are?"

Mason smirked.

"Royal blue is an excellent choice, sir. I have just the thing," the associate assured him, then looked him up and down as if he could measure him without tape. It made Henry decidedly uncomfortable, enough to make him want to squirm under the salesman's perusal.

"Did you have a specific coat cut in mind?"

Wasn't it enough that he had to choose a color? Now they were asking about cut, whatever that was?

"I have no idea."

"Let's go traditional," Mason said.

"Thank you," Henry said with a miserable groan.

"What kind of tie would you like to pair with your tuxedo, sir?" the associate asked, gesturing for Henry to follow him to a group of mannequins set up to display a number of different tie styles.

"Yeah, *sir*, what do you think?" Mason repeated. The older man was milking it for all he was worth.

"You're supposed to be helping," Henry reminded him with a nervous laugh. "What did Charli and her family say about what kind of tie I should choose?"

Mason shook his head. "Not a thing. Hang on and I'll text Charli."

While Mason had his nose in his phone, the salesman explained to Henry what he was looking at, everything from a traditional bow tie to regular and skinny neckties, to what the salesman called an ascot, which looked to Henry like old-fashioned English frippery.

He was drowning. He was really, truly drowning.

Was Charli feeling the same way right now?

There were way too many choices, and as far as ties were concerned, Henry didn't really like any of them. He never wore ties, and he already felt as if he were choking without even wrapping the fabric around his neck.

"She says don't worry about a tie for now," Mason said, approaching Henry and the salesman. "You own a decent bolo, right, Henry?"

"Yeah. More than one. I wear my best one to church. It has an American bald eagle on it."

"Good enough. The ladies said you ought to pair a bolo with a tuxedo shirt. Charli said you'll look handsome that way." Mason winked at Henry.

Though he didn't have any bolo ties on display, the salesman was clearly used to customers requesting them as an option in a Montana town so deeply mired in the Old West. He led Henry into the changing room, where he left him to try on the tuxedo, mentioning that he would also have a few choices in cuff links when Henry emerged.

"Mason, will you please pick the cuff links for me?" Henry asked, feeling weary of choices and all decisioned out. He'd had no idea when he'd accepted Charli's proposal that he'd signed up for so much.

When he had on the tux, he just stared at his reflection for a moment, slack-jawed. Wearing a tuxedo was a far cry from his usual casual western wear. He hardly looked like the same man.

"Are you coming out here, or do I have to go in to see you?" Mason called with a laugh.

He didn't want to go on display before Mason, but he knew it was inevitable. Face flaming, Henry stepped out so Mason could officially give him a hard time, which he knew for sure was what was going to happen.

Instead, however, when Henry stepped out of the changing room, Mason lifted his eyebrows and gave a low whistle. He whirled his finger in a circular motion. "Not bad. Turn around so I can see the whole package."

Grimacing, Henry lifted his arms to shoulder level and did as Mason had asked, spinning on the balls of his socked feet and feeling very much as if he was doing a silly little ballet dance in front of his old friend.

Mason framed his white bearded chin between his thumb and forefinger. "Not bad. Not bad at all," he repeated.

"Really?" Henry asked hopefully, while inside he was wondering if Mason was just trying to talk him up to raise his confidence level.

"Really. Charli is going to flip when she sees you in all that royal blue. See?" Mason pushed him toward a three-way mirror.

Henry had to admit Mason was right. Henry barely recognized himself.

And the color really did bring out the blue in his eyes.

Chapter Twelve

Charli selected two of her gentlest horses for her sisters, haltered them and led them into the corral. She secured them next to Percy, who was already tacked up and prepared for the ride. Henry followed with his chestnut mare and an additional horse for Martha.

Charli was the most nervous she'd been since her mom and sisters had arrived in Hope, even more than when she'd presented her plan to save the ranch, if that were possible. Today was do or die. Make it or break it.

Today Martha, Fiona and Cordelia would get a glimpse into her heart. They could very easily reject her ranch—reject *her*. Not see what she saw, feel what she felt when she looked at this beautiful, productive land.

She was aware of Henry's gaze on her, and she turned to face him. With Levi being watched by Mason and the dogs running around his heels, he was leaning his forearms across his saddle, his expression thoughtful.

She narrowed her eyes on him. "Wha-a-at?" She drew out the question, a tingle running across her skin and leaving gooseflesh in its wake. Henry had always known her better than anyone, and ever since she'd proposed to him, she felt as if her connection with him was growing closer by the day.

He knew what she was thinking before she even spoke the words. He anticipated the feelings in her heart and the emotions swirling in her gut.

Henry was a simple, straightforward man in the best of senses, and she sent up a quick prayer of thanks for his presence by her side. Only with him would she be able to get through what could be a tough day.

"I know this is an important day for us. You look nervous."

"Rats. Do I really? And here I wanted to look calm, cool, smooth and sophisticated." She made a face, only half joking.

"You know I've got your back, right? In this and in everything." His voice had dropped and thickened with emotion.

"I know. I'm just not sure this is a good idea. I'm second-guessing myself."

"Trust me. It's a good idea," Henry replied. "This is your opportunity to prove your point in a visual way. Not only for them to see the beauty of the land itself, but how much it means to you. Kind of like the way Fiona named the cows."

Charli rolled her eyes. "Well, good or bad, it's too late to back out now. In for a penny, and all that." She gestured up to the ranch house, where her mom and sisters had emerged and were now walking down the hill toward the stable, her two sisters chatting as usual. "Here they come."

Not surprisingly, Fiona's voice was loud enough for the horses to become skittish—not a great start to the day. Martha appeared to realize this and said something to Fiona, who then clapped her hand over her mouth in dismay. Cordelia was holding back, clearly still uncertain about this whole endeavor.

Charli approached them, forcing a smile. "Everybody ready for today?"

Martha nodded, actually looking enthusiastic about the trail ride.

Fiona let out a squeak of exclamation and then promptly clamped her hand back over her mouth again, but her shiny-eyed gaze told it all. She was definitely up for new experiences, including a trail ride.

Cordelia, on the other hand, was shaking her head, her eyes wide and frightened.

"Have you ever ridden a horse before?" Charli asked Cordelia, thinking that perhaps she'd had a poor equine experience that had left a bad taste in her mouth.

"No," Cordelia admitted. "It's just that I have a hard time imagining being on the back of one of those gigantic animals."

"I think if you go in with an open mind, you'll find you'll bond with your horse." This surprising statement came from Martha before Charli could answer. "They may be big, but they're gentle."

"And Charli has picked the gentlest of the herd for you, a bay gelding named Poco," Henry said.

Relief flashed across Cordelia's expression. "Poco. That means small, right?"

Charli cringed inwardly.

Not exactly.

Poco was actually a draft horse and the largest in their stable, but while he was perhaps farther off the ground than the other mounts, he truly had the softest heart toward his riders and seemed to instinctively understand his rider's abilities. Poco was the horse she used with children unused to riding, and Charli was positive he was the right mount for Cordelia.

"Which one's mine?" Fiona asked, clearly trying to keep her voice from rising and scaring the horses.

Charli laughed. "Fittingly, I've chosen you an Appaloosa gelding named Happy." There could seriously not be a better pairing between horse and woman if Charli had tried. The gelding held his moniker for a reason. She'd never met a friendlier horse, which was why she'd added him to her stable.

"Which one is he?" Fiona asked.

Charli pointed to Happy, and once again, Fiona had to fight from displaying her excitement. "My horse has polka dots! Happy the Appy. Happaloosa."

"Lord, grant me the serenity," Charli mumbled under her breath. "Mom, you've got the palomino mare. Her name is Dolce."

Martha immediately strode up to her horse's head, patting the side of Dolce's neck and then running a hand down her muzzle. "Hello, Dolce. And what does your name mean?"

"Sweet," Henry said, speaking for the first time.

Not the pairing Charli would have given Martha, but Henry had insisted. Unlike her sisters, her mother was an experienced horsewoman, or at least she had been back in the day. Charli remembered her mom going on daily rides, and she wondered if there was a tiny part of her that missed having horses.

She supposed she'd see today.

With Martha and Fiona getting to know their mounts, Charli spent a few minutes with Cordelia, helping her get over her fear of Poco. As she'd expected, Poco held still for Cordelia to touch him and wasn't skittish even when the other horses appeared to be ready to hit the trail.

"Should we all get going?" Henry asked. "We have an old tree stump we use as a mounting block."

"You and Charli haven't introduced us to your mounts," Martha reminded them, though Charli couldn't imagine why that was of any interest to her mother. "Or your dogs, Henry. I've seen them running around the ranch."

"I ride a gray Arabian gelding named Percy," Charli said. "Sir Percy Blakeney is his full name, you know, from the hero in *The Scarlet Pimpernel*."

"That's clever. And you, Henry?" Martha pressed.

"Um...the dogs are named Red and Blue," he said, pointing to each one in turn. "They're both working cattle dogs. Well, Red is. I just got Blue a few weeks ago, and he's still learning the ropes. I'll kennel them for now or they'll try to follow us on the trail ride. Red would enjoy it, but Blue is still a little small."

Cordelia and Fiona tittered, and suddenly Charli could see where this line of questioning was bound to go. Alarm sirens went off in her mind, but she wasn't fast enough to avert the disaster she now saw coming.

Red and Blue, indeed.

"Red and Blue?" Martha asked, sounding incredulous. "You seriously named your dogs Red and Blue."

Henry lifted his eyebrows in surprise but completely without guile, feeling as if Martha was trying to belittle him. He wasn't stupid in any way, shape or form, as Charli kept reminding him. He was just a straightforward man. There was a difference. And he knew when people were making fun of him. Maybe it was because of all he'd experienced in his childhood, but he didn't like to make things any harder than they needed to be.

But right now he felt as if he were being cornered. Martha's lips were pursed, and Charli's sisters were looking at him as if he was an idiot. He recognized those expressions. He'd spent his whole life fighting them.

He straightened his shoulders and braced for whatever was coming next. In order not to have to face Martha straight on, he focused on tightening the cinch on his chestnut quarter horse's saddle. Charli stepped nearer to him under the guise of asking him a question, but Henry knew it was because she was also expecting some kind of scene to explode between him and her family.

Not if he could help it. He knew how to be the better man. Stay quiet. Don't react no matter what kind of nonsense came out of Martha's mouth. If he laughed at himself, it didn't matter whether they were laughing at him or with him. He wouldn't let it bother him.

"Hmm," said Martha. "So let me get this straight. If you've got Red and Blue for your dogs, I suppose your horse is named...*what*? Brownie?"

Wow. That was a crack shot if he'd ever heard one. It was also wrong.

And Charli scoffed in derision. "Guess again. His horse's name is Slappy."

"Slappy?" Martha echoed in disbelief. Fiona and Cordelia laughed. "What kind of a name is that?"

Charli grinned in satisfaction, her eyes shining with delight. "Henry, why don't you and Slappy do your thing and school these ladies on how to choose the right name for your animal?"

Henry's face warmed, but he saw where Charli was going with this and turned to Slappy, getting his attention with a couple of fond pats on his neck. "Give it a go, Slappy. Show everyone what makes you special."

Then he nodded, and the horse followed suit, vigorously tossing his head up and down. He suspected this movement would have been cute enough on its own, but Slappy's nodding wasn't the funny part, or the reason he'd earned his moniker. As Slappy moved, he loosened his big lips until they were literally slapping each other with each up and down motion.

Smack. Smack. Smack.

The horse's antics delighted the ladies, who all laughed and clucked, the sounds now genuine. Henry's heart warmed as much as his face had moments before, but this time it was the rich sound of Charli's laughter that moved him rather than the embarrassment he'd felt with her mom and sisters.

"See?" Charli said, sounding justified. "Slappy. Would you have named him anything different? I don't think so. Anyway, we ought to head out onto the trail."

Henry admired the way she took the lead, especially given that it was her family, and he knew how much influence they had over her and how nervous she was inside. "Henry, if you can help the ladies mount up, I'd like to spend a few more minutes with Cordelia and Poco helping them get to know each other."

Henry intended to lead the horses one at a time up to the mounting block, but only Fiona needed assistance into the saddle. Quick as a flash, Martha mounted Dolce without help, as if she'd been doing it all her life. It had to have been years since she'd been on a horse, but Henry knew she'd been born and raised in Hope. He suspected riding a horse must be every bit as easy as learning to ride a bike—something you didn't forget how to do. He grinned as he watched Martha put Dolce through her paces around the corral. Dolce had a responsive, soft mouth, and Martha sat straight in the saddle with her heels down in the stirrups. Henry was immediately impressed with her horsemanship.

He held the Appaloosa's bridle and guided Fiona as she threw her leg over and adjusted her seat in the saddle. She appeared as happy as her horse's name and wasn't afraid of being on a horse, even when Henry adjusted her stirrups to meet her short legs.

"How do I drive this guy?" Fiona asked as Henry showed her how to hold the reins. Before Henry could answer, Martha pulled Dolce up next to her. "Don't worry about it, Henry. I'll take over Fiona's *driving* lessons," she said, looking as if she was honestly enjoying herself. "Why don't you go help Charli convince Cordelia her horse isn't going to eat her."

He shook his head and chuckled under his breath, expecting that was probably just about what Charli was facing right now. He approached the ladies, who were both standing at the horse's head. Charli was trying to coax Cordelia into feeding Poco a treat. To the horse's credit, Poco wasn't moving at all, seeming to sense Cordelia needed extra care and attention.

"Are you sure he won't bite me?" Cordelia asked.

"He'll gently nibble against your palm. You know the way Slappy moved his lips? Poco will wiggle his lips the same way. Do you want Henry to show you how? That way if Poco takes off any fingers, it'll be his."

"Gee, thanks," he said with a laugh, already holding his hand out flat so Charli could place a treat on it.

Poco was the mellowest horse in their stable and used his lips to pull the treat into his mouth, just as Henry and Charli both expected.

Cordelia looked only marginally more convinced, but

she put out a shaky hand, swallowing nervously. Charli must have noticed Cordelia's tremor, as well, because she pressed her hand under Cordelia's in support before placing the treat on her palm.

Cordelia's eyes widened when the horse reached for the treat. "It tickles," she said, half in awe, half giggling.

"See? I knew you'd get along. Now you're friends," Charli announced in a cheery voice that Henry thought was a bit much for her. She was trying really hard to make a go of this.

"Is everyone else mounted?" she asked Henry.

"Your mom didn't even need the mounting block, much less any help from me," he said. "She's an amazing horsewoman."

"I remember watching her ride when I was young," she said. "And Fiona? How's she doing?"

He laughed. "All set to go. I had to adjust her stirrups. Her legs are so short."

"I guess it's your turn," Charli said, turning to Cordelia. "What do you think? Are you ready to get to know Poco better on a trail ride? I promise it's gonna be fun, and I'll never be far away from you."

Cordelia took a deep breath and nodded. "I think so. Just show me what to do."

"Of course," Charli said. "Let's get you up on the mounting block."

Henry led Poco over to the mounting block, and Charli held Cordelia's hand to help her stand upon it.

"Hold on to the saddle horn while you swing your right leg over, then balance yourself while we adjust the stirrups."

Cordelia didn't have any problems mounting, but she sat with her spine poker straight and clenched the saddle horn with white knuckles while Henry and Charli adjusted the stirrups. She didn't even look as if she was breathing.

"Can you feel him breathing under you? Try to use your knees and heels to balance rather than the saddle horn." Henry handed her the reins. "Hold them loose but not too loose," he instructed.

Once again, Martha took over, teaching her youngest daughter how to ride.

Soon Levi would be taking rides with them as they built a family together. It was exciting to think that she'd have the blessing of being able to watch Levi grow up here on the ranch, her little cowboy.

It was something they needed to address, sooner rather than later.

But not right now.

"Why don't you lead out, and I'll drop back to the end to make sure everyone is doing okay," Henry suggested.

"Good idea. Keep an eye out in case anything goes wrong."

Henry chuckled. "Nothing's going to go wrong, Charli."

"Says you." She let out a sigh. "I'll be glad when this day is over."

"Try to enjoy yourself," he suggested.

"Right," she said, her voice tight. "Enjoy myself. Woo-hoo. Can't wait."

He grinned and shook his head. She took everything so seriously. He felt for her. He also found her amusing.

But most of all, he believed in her. Today would go well.

Chapter Thirteen

In a chain of nose-to-tail horses, Charli kept Percy at a slow walk as they crossed field after field in single file. Charli was followed by Cordelia, Martha, Fiona and finally Henry. Charli knew the placid Poco would follow Percy without issue, but she made sure her headstrong, spirited mount didn't take off in the gallop he wanted to.

Martha suddenly pulled off to the side and trotted forward until Dolce was side by side with Percy. Charli glanced back to make sure Cordelia was still okay, but Poco was plodding along just fine.

Martha was laughing. Charli had always thought her mother was beautiful, but seeing her smile made all the difference in the world. She was beaming with delight.

"I know we're just going on a trail ride today," her mom said, "but before we head into the forest, do you think I could take a little detour for a quick gallop across the field? I haven't had the opportunity to ride in years, and my heart is just aching to add some speed to our outing. And I'm pretty sure Dolce is feeling me."

As if in agreement, Dolce tossed her head and neighed, causing both Martha and Charli to laugh.

"Sure. Go ahead," Charli said. It wasn't as if she could

tell her mother no. That would just be weird. "Be careful, though," she added as an afterthought.

She didn't need to say anything. Martha clicked her tongue and turned Dolce out toward the field, and the next moment they were at a full gallop, her mother leaning forward over her horse's neck and urging her on. Suddenly she made a quick turn, then heeled the horse forward again, making another quick turn, heading farther away and making a tight third turn before heading back toward the waiting group at breakneck speed.

Charli thought she was magnificent.

Martha whooped as she pulled up, her cheeks flushed with exhilaration.

"You were a barrel racer?" Henry asked.

"Yep. From the time I was in junior high. I also did team roping with my best friend. Not to brag or anything, but I was pretty good, if I do say so myself. This was so fun."

Charli had to clamp her mouth shut so her jaw didn't hit the ground. Ever since her mom had arrived back in Hope, she'd dressed and acted like a city living highflyer in expensive blouses and purses that no doubt cost more than Charli's best pair of boots and hat combined. To think of her as a country girl just didn't match up with the woman she now was.

"I have to say I'd forgotten what a heart pumping ride galloping on a horse can be," Martha stated, taking a deep breath. "And the fresh air. I have to admit I've missed it."

Charli turned her gaze to Henry, who winked at her and flashed a charming half smile. Things were going better than she ever could have anticipated. Now, as long as Cordelia continued to get along with Poco, they might actually succeed in convincing her family about how important this ranch was to them.

"This is breathtakingly beautiful," Fiona said as Charli led the small group into the pines and aspens.

"Isn't it, though?" Charli agreed. "It's called Big Sky for a reason. I can't imagine living anywhere else. I look around me and see the Creator's hand in everything."

A red-tailed hawk caught the breeze above them, gently sailing on its broad wings. A squirrel chattered at them from a nearby tree.

"Keep a lookout for deer," Henry said. "We have a herd that likes to hang around in the brush."

Cordelia really hadn't said much, which had initially worried Charli, but she appeared to be enjoying herself, or at least not hating the ride outright.

A few minutes later, they approached the picnic area, where several years ago Henry and her father had built a picnic table, a hitching post and a firepit. It wasn't used much, but Charli was glad to have it now.

"I thought we'd stop for a rest and have a bite to eat," Charli said as she dismounted and loosened Percy's cinch before tying him to the hitching post.

"What a nice surprise," said Martha, also dismounting. She didn't need assistance loosening the girth or tying her mare to the hitching post, either. Apparently, it wasn't just her riding that had come back to her, but caring for her horse as well.

"I could eat," Fiona agreed.

"Do you have any water? I'm dying of thirst," Cordelia said.

Henry had also already dismounted and moved to Poco's side, assisting Cordelia in her dismount.

Charli thought Cordelia may have had all she wanted of horses, but she moved to Poco's head and patted his neck affectionately, cheerily talking to him.

"So, what do you think?" Henry asked. "Are you and Poco getting along?"

Charli was wondering the exact same thing but wasn't about to ask the question aloud for fear of the answer.

"I don't know why I was so afraid," she said, stroking Poco's muzzle. "I guess because horses just seemed so large, and I was afraid I would fall off because I'm something of a klutz to begin with. My equilibrium isn't always the greatest. Of course, we're only walking the horses and not doing the crazy riding like Mama was doing, but I didn't have any trouble staying in the saddle."

"You can learn to ride faster if you want," Martha said. "I can show you how. Or I'm sure Charli or Henry will teach you if you'd rather learn from someone who has actually been riding in the last decade or so."

"Oh, don't be shy," Charli said, shaking her finger at her mom. "You remember a whole lot more than you were letting on. Incredible riding."

"I might be interested in learning more," Cordelia said in a moderated, thoughtful tone. "If I was staying around long enough to take lessons. But I'm not sure what I'm doing yet. A lot is still up in the air."

That statement was like a punch to Charli's gut, and she struggled not to react.

"Count me in. I want to learn!" Fiona jumped in with her usual unique brand of enthusiasm, where every sentence sounded as if it ended in an exclamation point. "I'm almost positive I'm going to be sticking around Hope. If I'm going to live here, I definitely need to know how to ride a horse!"

"Well, it's not as if everyone in town still rides horses down Main Street," Henry said with a laugh. "Although there is an old hitching post and water trough in front of the general store that no one ever bothered to remove."

"And I noticed all the men wear cowboy hats everywhere they go," Fiona pointed out.

Charli chuckled, not correcting her of the notion that every man who wore a cowboy hat rode horses. "Not just the men. Many women also prefer to wear cowboy hats. But yeah, the cowboy hats and boots are still a big part of our western culture in Hope."

"Works for me," Fiona said dreamily. "I've gotta say I think cowboys are hunky and handsome."

For once, Charli actually agreed with Fiona. There was one particular cowboy who was especially handsome, in her opinion.

"What do you think, Cordelia?" Charli asked.

"I don't know. I've always gone for the CEO type in suits, but that obviously hasn't gone so well for me. I've heard cowboys are kind and honest, so maybe I've been looking for love in all the wrong places."

Martha snorted. "Get your heads out of the clouds, girls. It takes a lot more than a hat and boots to make a man worthy of any of you. You have to find a man with heart."

"I've found one," Charli said, flashing Henry a cheeky smile and a coy wink. "Henry is everything a woman could want in a man."

His face immediately heated so hot he was certain steam must be coming out of his ears, and his heart hammered so hard he was sure all the ladies could hear it as they turned to look at him with inquiring gazes. Were they going to make fun of him for Charli's off-the-cuff remark?

But no. Their smiles weren't jeering or unkind.

"I don't think we've properly welcomed you and Levi to the family, Henry," Martha said after an extended and—at least for Henry—very uncomfortable silence.

"I, er, thank you. There is no one I would rather be marrying than Charli." That, at least, was the truth, even if she didn't know it.

"I think we should eat." Charli jumped into the conversation, practically babbling, and Henry guessed she hadn't exactly planned to go down this rabbit hole, either. He agreed wholeheartedly and joined her in unpacking their lunch fare from the saddlebags.

Charli spread a tablecloth across the picnic table with her mother's help and laid everything out. "What we've basically got here," Charli said, "is a charcuterie board without the board. It's the Wild West, after all, so we've opted for paper plates instead."

Henry had helped her prepare the food earlier that day. Deli-sliced ham and turkey, slices of sharp cheddar and Swiss cheese, tomatoes, lettuce and hoagie buns. They had packets of mayo and mustard, as well as dill pickles and sliced apples. He carried an armful of still-cold water bottles to the table.

Conversation came surprisingly easily for everyone. Even Charli was chiming in from time to time.

Charli leaned in close to him.

"You want to take a walk?"

"Sure."

The area around the picnic spot was familiar to both of them, so Henry took her hand, lacing their fingers, and walked toward a nearby creek at a slow, leisurely pace. Though he wanted to find out what was on Charli's mind that had her looking so thoughtful, Henry didn't feel the need to speak right away, so they walked in silence for a while, just enjoying the mild weather and the sunshine.

With the mutual regard of many years of friendship, they automatically stopped together along the edge of the creek underneath the shade of a large aspen tree and turned to face one another.

"Today is going well, I think," Henry said, grabbing on to a branch over his head with both hands to stretch out the muscles in his back and shoulders. "Your family appears to me to be less...hostile than they were when they first got here. I think they may be starting to see things your—*our* way."

"I know, right?" Henry hadn't heard Charli this excited in—well, ever, maybe. "I really think they may be reconsidering their point of view about us keeping the ranch, and they've all grown to love Levi already. I never thought I'd see my mom take off on her horse like that at a straight gallop. She's a real pro, and she was genuinely stoked about it. I never even knew she participated in rodeo."

"Yeah, I wouldn't have guessed it, either," Henry agreed. "Not with how she usually dresses."

He was genuinely happy about how things appeared to be working out where the ranch was concerned, but he'd also been thinking of the way Martha's attitude had warmed regarding him. He wondered if Charli had noticed that, or if she was only thinking of her ranch. "And if she had done rodeo, which seems so foreign to the person she appeared to be now, I would have pegged her for a princess, not a barrel racer and roper."

Charli giggled. Henry wasn't sure he'd ever heard her giggle before. She didn't even laugh that often, but now she was as full of joy as he'd ever seen her.

And that filled his heart with joy.

"Even Cordelia seemed to enjoy the ride. Can you believe it?" she said. "I never expected her to change her opinion on horses."

And then she did something so un-Charli that it took Henry completely by surprise. She rushed up to him and threw her arms around his neck, so quickly that her cowboy hat flew off her head and flopped to the ground unnoticed. "I'm so happy."

Henry froze, afraid even the tiniest movement would break this moment, the feeling of her arms around him, her warm breath against his cheek.

He didn't want it to end.

"Me, too," he agreed, his voice husky and a good octave lower than usual. "I'm so glad you're going to get what you've worked so hard for, Charli. No one is more deserving than you to win this one."

Their eyes locked and held, and he read something deep and unnameable in her inscrutable blue depths. She curled her fingers into the hair at the back of his neck with one hand, while the other tipped up the front brim of his hat before slowly trailing down his shoulder to hover over his chest, where her palm rested on his heart. Surely she could feel the frantic way it hammered under her touch.

"Henry?" she asked in a soft hum.

He leaned down at the same time as she rose to her tiptoes, and before he realized what was happening, his lips were gently brushing hers—once and then twice before settling over them. Her mouth was soft and giving, and he responded in kind, wanting her to know what he was feeling, that he was offering her his whole heart. His life. Telling her everything he hadn't been able to say in words the only way he could.

His hands dropped to frame her face as they broke the kiss, their foreheads touching as each simply felt the emotions suspended between them. He had waited so very long for this moment. How many times had he dreamed of kissing her, of holding her close?

And now they had a lifetime to make those dreams a reality.

"Oh, I'm so sorry!" It was Fiona's voice, and Charli jumped out of Henry's arms as if she'd suddenly been electrocuted by him, trembling as she stood there staring as if he was Frankenstein's monster.

He stared back and forth between the two women, not really sure what was happening but knowing something was very wrong with this picture.

If he was honest, his feelings were hurt. Yes, he and Charli had been sharing a private moment between them and hadn't expected to be interrupted, but they were engaged, after all. Was Charli really that embarrassed to be caught kissing him?

"I can leave and come back again if you want so I don't surprise you," Fiona suggested cheerfully and a little bit coyly. "I was just coming to let you know everyone is ready to head back to the ranch house."

"No, that's fine," Charli said a little too quickly and far too airily, scooping her hat off the ground and putting it back on her head in a rush. "We were just on our way back to you guys, anyway."

They hadn't been. Obviously. Henry's mind and heart

had been a million miles away from this little copse by the creek, and he definitely hadn't been thinking of returning to her family.

And now Charli was acting as if what had happened between them was nothing.

Henry's emotions were a wreck. How hard was it going to be for him to live with her as husband and wife if she didn't love him? He'd been questioning this all along, but this kiss changed everything. He knew she meant to be a true wife to him in every way, but theirs was a business arrangement, not true love, and there would always be that emotional barrier between them.

He had to pray about this. He'd been up and down on the subject so many times, and he'd already made his commitment. He wouldn't back out on her now no matter how he felt. And that was to say nothing of what Charli could bring to Levi's life. There was simply too much at stake here.

But how was he going to live his whole life this way?

Chapter Fourteen

Charli's mind was on autopilot as she tightened all the saddles and helped her sisters mount their horses. She didn't say anything more to Henry, but mounted Percy and took her place at the front of the line to lead the small group of equestrians home.

To say she was shaken by what had just happened was an understatement. She was overreacting big time. She knew that. And the crazy part was, she didn't even know why. Henry was her fiancé. Of course they'd kiss each other. There was nothing remotely strange about that. Fiona wouldn't have been shocked to have walked in on them in an embrace.

But for some reason she couldn't explain even to herself, she'd been shaken beyond belief when they'd been caught together. Part of it, she knew, was the kiss itself. She'd thought of what it would be like to kiss Henry. Often. Of course she had. She might not be sweet and feminine like her mom and sisters, but she wasn't made of stone. And Henry was special to her, more than she was perhaps willing to admit, even to herself. Charli didn't understand why she was acting so immature about her relationship with Henry all of a sudden.

Sometimes when she was out in the field herding cattle, her mind would wander to what his lips would feel like as they pressed against hers, as she brushed her palms against the scruff on his cheeks and combed her fingers into the soft curls at the back of his neck. And then, when it had really happened, she'd freaked out.

Maybe it was that Fiona had walked in on them when she was still trying to wrap her mind and heart around her feelings. She was a private person, and what she'd been sharing with Henry, their incredible first kiss, was most definitely private.

Though she was still trembling internally from the encounter, she tried to put it aside, at least for now, and focus on the present. She glanced back at Cordelia, who was sitting straight in her saddle and smiling as she interacted with her mount and took in the mountain scenery.

"You and Poco doing okay back there?" Charli asked.

"Oh, yes. I had no idea I'd enjoy this so much. I hope I have more time to spend with him before I leave."

"Well, since you're living in the ranch house right now, it'll be easy for you. You're welcome to visit Poco any time you want. I don't stable the horses, but the herd usually stays close to the house because that's where the food comes from, and where the water troughs are located."

"So I can just stand and watch the horses? That won't be a problem?"

"The more you interact with them, the closer you'll get. If you call Poco by name, he'll come to you at the fence."

"Well, I want to get to know this guy better, for sure," Cordelia said with a genuine smile. Charli had mostly seen her sister glowering, so she appreciated how pretty Cordelia's smile made her. She really was lovely. "I'm so glad you introduced us."

"Me, too."

Though the ride back to the ranch house was the same distance they'd traveled, the ride home seemed faster. They were still plodding at a slow pace, but not quite as leisurely as the way out now that Cordelia had had time to adjust to riding in the saddle and seemed to be catching on as well as Fiona. It was in their blood, after all. Her father had been in rodeo, as well, and was a lifetime rancher. It shouldn't be a surprise that their daughters were all naturals.

Charli just wanted to get home so she could do her evening chores and go to bed, where she would have the silence and hopefully the solace she needed to examine her emotions and pray about them, seeking God's guidance and hoping for answers to her confusion. She had to figure out what she was feeling—and fast. It wasn't as if she could avoid Henry even for a day on the ranch, and since they'd worked out wedding details with Pastor Thomas, including a three-week online premarital course, it wasn't going to be that long before they got married, which they'd decided would take place two weeks after the court date so they could give the judge an exact month and day. After that, they'd be living together as well as working together.

She couldn't run away from him, or the situation. And let's be honest.

She didn't want to. She had *liked* kissing Henry. She wanted to do it more.

A lot more.

But the butterflies, the loosey-goosey feelings flooding through her making her feel like a princess in a Disney cartoon? Those could go away right now, thank you. She had work to do, a ranch to run. She would not admit she kinda-sorta enjoyed those woo-woo feelings because she didn't have time for them.

They reached the ranch and got everyone dismounted, and Fiona and Cordelia went back to the house. With the horses tied to the rail, Charli finished removing tack from Poco and Happy and rubbed them down. She planned to give them each a bucket of oats before putting them back out with the herd since they'd all done so well today, and she was just coming out of the stable with feed buckets when she noticed her mom removing Dolce's saddle.

Henry saw Martha at the same time and rushed to her, reaching out to grab her arm. "We can do that for you, Martha. Why don't you go in and relax?"

She narrowed her gaze on Henry to a sizzle that caused him to move back a step. Charli wouldn't have wanted to have been on the receiving end of that stare.

"I was doing this when you were in diapers," she informed him, her sharp voice firmly back in place. "I am perfectly capable of taking care of Dolce all on my own."

Henry placed a hand over his heart. "Of course. My mistake."

Charli laughed softly. This new Martha was going to take some getting used to. She was so much more than what Charli had originally thought. It was nice getting to know this side of her mother.

Suddenly, in the middle of brushing Percy down and feeding him some oats, she froze, feeling something was wrong, an intense inner sense that had taken her through her many years of ranching. Without thinking further or questioning her gut, she turned to where Henry was getting ready to unsaddle Slappy.

His eyebrows lowered when he saw her. "What's wrong?"

"I don't know. I…do you smell something?"

He frowned and paused. "Smoke?"

Without another word, they ran around the side of the barn toward the ranch house, but everything looked fine. It was only when they turned around to the other corner of the stable that they saw the blaze. Though her herd remained in the pasture year round, a lean-to that was generally used as an extra place for her dozen horses to find shade in the summer or shelter against winter storms, had recently been loaded with hay bales by day laborers. Thankfully, there were only a few bales stacked there and the land around the area was well-trampled by the horses, but the fire was still a serious issue.

Apparently Martha had smelled the smoke, as well.

"Fire," she yelled just as Henry and Charli broke into a run toward the barn where the fire extinguisher was kept.

Henry reached for Charli's arm as she picked up the heavy red metal container. "I'm going to grab some tarps," he said through gritted teeth. "I'll be right behind you."

Charli nodded and ran full speed toward the lean-to. Martha was already there, her hands on her hips and her lips pursed in thought as she stared at the disaster that had once been a shelter.

"Thank the good Lord, the fire appears to be containing itself. I think if we keep an eye on it, it will burn out on its own," Charli's mom told her. "The lean-to will have to be rebuilt, but it was smart of you to keep the grass low around it. And at least there were no horses around to get injured."

Charli nodded but decided it wouldn't hurt to use the fire extinguisher to try to get the fire under better control. She cringed even as she wrestled with the fire extinguisher, something she'd never had reason to use before. Fortunately, she'd seen it done enough on television, and it was a simple process. She pulled the pin to open the extinguisher, then pointed and sprayed back and forth over the flames. At first, she spread it across the top but found it wasn't very effective, so she shifted the heavy extinguisher to help her spray the fire closer to the ground.

"I've got the tarps," said an out-of-breath Henry as he ran up behind her, his arms loaded with canvas. "Hold off on the spray for a moment and let me throw a few of these on the open flames."

Charli stepped back with a sigh, anger and frustration roiling through her gut. How could this have happened?

The tarps worked well and quickly extinguished the fire, leaving only smoldering ashes. It turned out to be a fairly small, contained fire, but the lean-to would need some work before it would be safe for the horses again.

"How do you suppose it happened?" Henry mused, taking off his black cowboy hat and scratching the back of his neck. "It doesn't make sense."

Martha frowned and walked around the area, studying it carefully. "Did you have the bales up on blocks?" she asked. "Was the hay maybe wetter than you realized? And how closely was it stacked together? Hay bales can spontaneously combust in certain circumstances, you know."

It didn't exactly sound like judgment, but then again, even if Martha wasn't judging her, Charli was judging herself.

How could she have been so stupid?

"I always double-check…" Charli paused, then swallowed hard. "I honestly don't know. We usually only bale and store our own hay, but a neighbor was moving and asked if we wanted a few extra bales for a good price. Our cattle are always hungry, and I wasn't going to pass up cheap hay."

"But we didn't see to storing it ourselves. We used our neighbor's day laborers to move and set the hay," said Henry, picking up the story. He moved to Charli's side, taking her hand and giving it a reassuring squeeze. It helped her to know she wasn't facing this alone.

"I meant to come up and check on it, but things just got so…busy." She finished the explanation lamely, her face heating. She'd had so many things going on, the truth was checking the extra hay had just slipped her mind. She never imagined it would explode. She thanked God no human or animal had been hurt. But even though they'd only lost a few bales of hay and would have to rebuild the lean-to, and though it could have been so much worse except for the grace of God, the fire was still her responsibility.

Where her ranch was concerned, the buck stopped with her.

Henry waited to talk to Charli until Martha had gone back to the ranch house. He knew Charli well enough—she was carrying the world on her shoulders, an emotional load no one should bear on their own, and he hoped to remind her she didn't have to do that anymore. Whatever they had to face they would conquer together.

Charli sighed deeply. "Well, that was a new and unusual experience. What a horrible end to the day."

She wasn't usually sarcastic, which only made Henry worry all the more.

"I guess we should check on the horses and let them out with the herd before we leave for the evening," he suggested gently, as much to get her mind on something other than the fire as that the horses actually needed attention. Plus, he could use their few minutes of privacy in the barn to reassure her everything was going to be okay.

"Yeah, I suppose we should."

Henry's heart hurt for her. She sounded absolutely miserable, and he knew why—because she blamed herself for what had happened this afternoon. Odd how just hours earlier his biggest worry had been the weirdness they'd experienced after they'd shared a wonderful kiss together. Now the fire had totally eclipsed that.

Honestly, he wasn't sure whether that was a good thing or a bad thing.

Henry followed her into the barn and reached for the bag of oats, shaking some into two buckets and walking back out before handing one to Charli so she could feed the horses still tied on the corral fence.

He glanced over his shoulder to find Charli feeding Percy, her forehead leaning against her horse's muzzle, her hat brim curled in her fist. Her whole body was slumped in agonizing defeat.

He tried to speak but his words came out husky. He cleared his throat. "It wasn't your fault, you know," he said gently. "You can't blame yourself for what happened."

Charli turned to him, her expression agonized. "How do you figure?"

"It was just a random accident," he said. "No one could have predicted it."

Charli slid to the floor, her back against the fence and her hat dropping to the ground.

"My mom noticed the problem right away. There were no blocks there, Henry. Any ranch hand worth his salt knows to put hay bales on blocks, especially if there's any moisture in it."

"Maybe they weren't ranch hands?" he suggested tentatively. "They may have just been regular day laborers who didn't know any different."

"Don't you understand? It doesn't matter if they were or weren't!" She practically snapped his head off.

"Whoa." He held up his hands palms outward. "Hold on a minute, sweetheart. I'm on your side."

She took a deep breath and exhaled loudly. "I'm sorry. You didn't deserve that. My point is that if I was doing my job correctly, this wouldn't have happened. I should have checked that load weeks ago. It's just that everything changed about that time, and I forgot about it. But that's absolutely no excuse. It's all on me."

"It is *not* all on you. Don't you dare do that to yourself." Henry crouched before her and lifted her face to his, forcing their gazes to meet. He wanted to be absolutely certain she understood what he was about to say, that his words went heart deep. "Listen to me. We are engaged. And we run this ranch—*our* ranch—together. I had the intention of checking that load and didn't get around to it, either. I'm every bit as culpable as you are. Why aren't you blaming me?"

"Henry. No." She reached out and pressed her palm to his cheek. For a moment he closed his eyes and leaned into her touch.

"I agree that we would have seen the potential problem if either or both of us would have checked," he said. "And no amount of whirlwind changes should have knocked us for a loop. But Charli, can't you see how God was watching over us? No one was hurt, and I can easily rebuild the lean-to. No real harm was done. We should be grateful."

"I know I should be grateful to God it wasn't worse, but I'm not so sure there was no harm done. Did you see my mother's face?"

"She knows her stuff," he had to admit. "She put the problem together before either of us did."

"She grew up on a ranch," Charli said with a groan. "And then she lived on this one until she and Dad got divorced. She probably thinks I'm totally incapable of running a ranch now. And I've just proven it to her, haven't I?"

Henry rose and drew Charli to her feet, pulling her into his arms. He thought after this afternoon that she might resist, but she didn't. She curled into him, pressing her cheek into his shoulder.

"I don't believe that. She grew up on a ranch. She knows how many things are out of our control, how much is in God's hands. And no matter how hard we work, there's always more to do."

"I'll have to face her eventually," she said, burying her face in his shoulder. "But not yet."

"I guess it's a good thing we have court this week, then," Henry reminded her, not that it would have slipped her mind. He was certain she was as cognizant of it as he was. "We have an excuse to avoid her, at least for now. By the time we see her again, maybe she'll have forgotten all about it."

Of course she wouldn't forget about something as big as a fire. And they both knew it. But Henry was right about one thing, and his gut tightened just thinking about it.

Court was next week.

Chapter Fifteen

Henry looked as if he was about to choke, but Charli didn't know if it was because he was wearing his Sunday best navy suit with a matching straight blue tie or because they were in the parking lot of the court getting ready to enter and speak to a judge. She thought he was quite handsome in his suit, though truthfully she preferred him in old jeans and his hat and boots. At least she got to wear her cowboy boots, albeit her good pair, along with a nice blouse and an ankle-length flowing skirt in a wildflower pattern.

As uncomfortable as he clearly was with his outfit, Charli knew he was feeling ten times more awkward than that in his mind. Levi was sound asleep on Henry's shoulder, but it almost looked as if the large man was clinging to the baby boy. Charli had suggested bringing in the car seat, but Henry wanted to hold the baby in his arms. Maybe to show the judge he looked like a father?

Or maybe it was for moral support.

Today was the big day when Levi's guardianship would be determined. In just a few hours they would know if they would get to keep the baby. Guardianship was the first step toward becoming Levi's parents, a thought that, while still daunting, was a little less so than when they'd first received the baby out of nowhere a few weeks ago. It was amazing how fast a person could adapt when push came to shove.

And where there was love.

They walked into the courthouse together and went through security, then checked the docket to find out which courtroom they'd be in. After that, it was a matter of consulting the map on the wall to figure out where they were going.

"You'd think they could make this a little easier," Henry muttered under his breath. "I imagine most everyone is nervous when they come here to start with. Why make it even more complicated?"

"We've got this," Charli said. "Come on. I've always been good with maps."

They went up a staircase, around a corner and then up another winding, open staircase to the third floor.

"I think there's a hallway around here somewhere. That's where the family courtrooms are supposed to be. We're in Courtroom 311."

They turned one more corner and found the hallway they were looking for. The courtrooms were located on the left side, while a series of large windows on the right. In between each window was a decorated bench.

"This is 305," Charli said, looking at the first door. "So 311 should be just down this way."

She started to walk forward but turned around when she realized Henry wasn't with her. He was standing frozen in place, his face as white as a sheet.

This was no time for him to get a case of nerves. Their lawyer was supposed to be waiting for them, and she wanted to have time to go over their notes before they went into the courtroom.

"Henry?" she said, tentatively approaching him and wondering at the best way to calm him down.

"She's here," he hissed under his breath. "She's not supposed to be here."

"What? Who is here?" She turned around to try to figure out who he was looking at that had disturbed him so much. There were many people in the hallway, most of them buzzing about in small groups of two or three, but she didn't see anyone she recognized.

"Who?" she asked again.

"Jamie Lynn."

"Your sister is here?" she said, disbelief flooding through her. This was *not* supposed to be happening right now. There was only one reason Charli could think of that Jamie Lynn would be here today, and it wasn't good.

Then again, why would she wait until they were in court? Why not just contact Henry at the ranch if she wanted anything to do with her son? She knew where Henry lived—she'd left Levi at his cabin in the first place.

"I think the woman with her may be a lawyer," Henry said tightly. "What are we going to do, Charli?"

"Okay, let's not get ahead of ourselves." Charli tried to even out her breathing. "Let's just sit down here at the end of the hallway for a moment and wait for our turn to be called in. I'm sure if we stay seated Amber will find us. Jamie Lynn doesn't need to see you until then. As far as the woman with her goes, maybe she just brought a friend to support her."

"Should I go talk to her, do you think?" he asked.

"Do you want to?"

He sat squarely back in his seat, his pulse beating in the corner of his clenched jaw. "No. Absolutely not. What if she wants to take Levi away from us?"

"I see Amber now. I'll go talk to her and fill her in on what's going on. She'll probably want to go talk to Jamie Lynn and find out if that's her lawyer, and then she'll be able to give us an idea what to do from there. And Henry?"

He had buried his nose in the baby's hair, inhaling Levi's unique baby scent. Henry looked up at the sound of his name. Charli reached out and squeezed his hand.

"We've got this. Don't forget—we have everything we need to win guardianship of Levi. Your sister left him with us, and she as much as signed him over to us with the handwritten note. That's a major piece of evidence. Plus, she hasn't contacted us even once since to see how Levi was doing. No judge in his right mind would hand him back to Jamie Lynn. Not when Levi has a nice stable family—you and me."

She only hoped it was true.

Henry had actually convinced himself their day in court would be, if not easy, then at least straightforward. Now he felt as if everything was falling apart.

What if they lost Levi?

It had only been a short amount of time, yet Charli and Henry had bonded with Levi as if he were their own son. He'd been so certain this was God's plan for them. He loved the little baby in his arms.

Now, as he watched Charli animatedly speaking with their lawyer, he just felt emotionally wrecked. He wasn't sure how he was going to get through this day and offered a quick prayer thanking God for Charli's support.

"It's okay, baby boy," he said, more to reassure himself than Levi, who'd woken and was sitting in his lap slurping on the bottle Henry had offered. He was starting to eat solid foods now, but today they'd brought bottles of formula for backup and to keep Levi calm and quiet while they were in the courtroom.

A buzzer sounded, and people poured out of the courtrooms. For a second, Henry lost sight of Charli, and he felt a moment of panic, even knowing she was still there and that she would never leave him. He recognized once again how much he'd come to depend on her.

Suddenly, Charli was before him, their lawyer at her shoulder.

"Come on," she said, reaching for Levi. "It's time."

His heart thudding, he followed Amber and Charli into their courtroom. There were several family names listed on the large computer docket screen on the wall, and Henry realized theirs wasn't the only case the judge was hearing during this time period. Their lawyer directed them to sit on one of the seats facing the judge's bench. Other family groups were doing the same.

Jamie Lynn and the woman with her sat on the far side of the room. He watched her for a minute, but she didn't look at him, and he wondered again why she was here, the knot tightening in the pit of his stomach.

He was surprised by the layout of the courtroom. For one thing, the judge's bench was enormous, taking up almost the entire front wall. There were several monitors across the desk, and he wondered how the judge kept track of all the information contained on them. Also, there was no jury box. Evidently, in this courtroom, at least, judges made determinations without jury input.

There were two tables situated in front of the public seats and a podium with a microphone placed in the middle. If the circumstances weren't so dire, Henry might have been curious as to how all this worked. He'd never wanted to be anything but a cowboy, but he had a healthy respect for the justice system.

"All rise," the bailiff said, his voice echoing into a microphone clipped to his suit jacket. "This court with the Honorable Natalia Brown presiding is now in session. Please be seated and come to order."

There was no court reporter. Evidently, technology had caught up and taken the place of a person recording everything that was said and done in the courtroom.

Their case was third on a docket of six, but when the judge made her opening remarks, the woman with Jamie Lynn stood and approached the podium, introducing herself and Jamie Lynn and indicating they wanted to take part in the proceedings regarding Levi.

"We'll switch you to last on the docket," the judge informed them, then immediately proceeded to the first case.

So his sister did want to meddle in the court case and make things more difficult for Henry, Charli and Levi. Henry felt sick to his stomach. And now they'd have to wait even longer to have their case heard. His head was swirling.

"Do you have any idea what Jamie Lynn's going to say?" Henry asked Charli in a hoarse whisper.

Charli shook her head. "Amber was unable to go speak to your sister and her lawyer. The announcement of our docket time came too quickly. She told me not to worry about it, though."

"Easy for her to say," he said under his breath.

Charli bounced Levi against her shoulder. The baby was making small sounds, and Henry thought about taking him from Charli, but he was afraid Levi might start to wail if he did that. Babies could sense emotions, and Henry had experienced more than one time that Levi had responded in kind to how Henry was feeling.

At the moment, Henry wanted to growl in frustration. Instead, he took deep, slow breaths to calm himself. When he finally felt focused enough to take Levi, the baby was already asleep, happily curled in the crook of Charli's arms, so he left the sleeping babe where he was.

At least that was one less thing to worry about.

Chapter Sixteen

Though it couldn't have been more than an hour, it felt like forever to get through the cases before them until it was finally just their family left to go. Family after family had filed out, and the courtroom echoed with Amber's steps as she approached the podium. Charli tried not to tense her shoulders, since she was still holding the sleeping baby, but it was hard to stay relaxed.

As if it wasn't hard enough to remain undisturbed, next to her, Henry was an absolute mess. His spine was poker straight, and his white-knuckled fists clenched the bench so tightly his arms quivered. She reached out and laid a hand over his, reminding him that they were in this together.

Amber quickly ran down the situation for the judge, including not only that Henry was willing to take on guardianship, but that Charli was there, as well, to take on co-guardianship. Judge Brown took a moment to read Jamie Lynn's letter to Henry then was silent for a long moment.

"Henry Parker, will you please approach the podium?" Judge Brown finally said at last.

"Your Honor?" Henry said respectfully, then cleared his throat.

"I understand you wish to become Levi's permanent guardian?"

"Yes, ma'am. And my fiancée, Charli Stafford. We'll be getting married in a couple of weeks and will care for Levi together."

"Be that as it may, today we are looking only at your qualifications. If Ms. Stafford wishes to pursue guardianship in the future, she will have to do so at a later date."

What? Henry turned a panicked glance back at Charli. She felt an equal frisson of alarm zip up her spine, making her skin break out in gooseflesh. After everything they'd done, their plan had failed. Her presence in court was neither here nor there as far as the judge was concerned.

She met Henry's gaze, willing him to remain calm. He could still win this.

"I understand you have a home of your own and a full-time job. Is that correct?"

"Yes, Your Honor." The judge wouldn't be able to hear it, but Charli knew Henry's voice was low and tight from the strain.

"And you are the only blood relative willing to take on Levi's guardianship?"

"Yes, Your Honor. I am grateful for the opportunity to raise my nephew and intend to seek to adopt him."

"Thank you. You may sit down," Judge Brown informed him, then silently turned her attention to the computers before her and typed some notes.

"You've got this," Charli whispered to him when he sat down, and he wrapped his arm around her and pulled her close, his other hand stroking Levi's hair.

Charli held her breath, expecting the judge to make her

ruling, when all of a sudden Jamie Lynn and her lawyer approached the podium.

"Your Honor, this is Levi's birth mother and Henry's sister. She is the woman who wrote the note to Henry, and she would like to have the opportunity to address the court now, please."

Judge Brown narrowed her eyes on Jamie Lynn, then sighed and motioned for Jamie Lynn to speak.

"Please, no," Henry begged in a voice so low and agonized that only Charli could hear him.

Charli leaned in next to Henry's ear. "I can't imagine she could possibly have anything to say that would be in her favor."

"She's his mother," Henry choked out.

Charli tucked herself and Levi closer under the strength of Henry's arm and waited for Jamie Lynn to speak.

"I came here today to speak on my brother Henry's behalf, and on behalf of my son, Levi."

Henry's gut was roiling. As much as he loved his sister, Jamie Lynn was in no condition to be a good mother to Levi. What would he do if the judge remanded the baby back into his sister's care? How could he protect Levi if that happened?

Jamie Lynn turned toward Henry and gestured for him to come forward to join her at the podium. Henry flashed Charli another panicked glance, his heart hammering in his throat. This was his worst nightmare come to life.

"Pray hard," he whispered to Charli before going forward to stand by his sister.

"Jamie Lynn," he greeted her through gritted teeth,

clasping his hands in front of him. "What are you doing here?"

She flashed him a genuine smile that merely confused him. "You'll see."

She sounded almost playful, as if this was some kind of game and not one of the most important moments of his life. He didn't get it. Not at all.

"I wasn't in a good place when I left Levi with Henry," Jamie Lynn told the judge. "I've fought an addiction for many years, ever since I was in junior high school. I am in no position to raise my son. I intend to check myself into rehab, but it won't be the first time, and I have a history of relapsing.

"My brother, Henry, on the other hand, is the strongest yet most gentle man I've ever known. I can't emphasize enough how good he will be at raising Levi. I am so proud of the man he has become, and I know he will give so much to my son's upbringing. I know I didn't go about this the right way, but I'm begging you to allow Henry to raise Levi as his own."

Henry nearly lost a grip on his emotions. Tears burned in the backs of his eyes, and his throat closed around his breath. His mind whirled as hard as his emotions swirled in his chest. He couldn't keep up with what was happening.

"Thank you for offering your point of view, Ms. Parker," the judge said. "Mr. Parker, stop by the clerk's office to sign the guardianship papers. Court is adjourned."

By the time Henry had moved back to gather Charli and Levi and the baby's things, Jamie Lynn and her lawyer had left the courtroom.

"We need to catch up with her," Henry said urgently.

"You go," Charli said. "We'll catch up with you."

Henry bolted from the courtroom and immediately skidded to a stop, looking both ways down the hallway, but he didn't see his sister. His heart thudded as he chose to go down the way they'd come in, walking in long, fast strides to try to catch up with her.

Just when he thought he'd lost her, he glimpsed Jamie Lynn standing near the clerk's office, chatting with her lawyer. He hadn't often seen her sober in recent years, and she had a genuine smile on her face, especially when she noticed him coming toward her. His emotions stirred once again, and he barely restrained himself from shedding a tear or two.

Yet when he approached her, he stood awkwardly, feeling as if he wanted to hug her but not sure if he should. The decision was taken out of his hands when Jamie Lynn threw her arms around him and practically knocked him to the floor.

He chuckled. "Easy, there," he said, steadying them both.

"Thank you, thank you, thank you, thank you, thank you," she repeated over and over. "God bless you for taking Levi for me."

"Thank *you*," Henry returned, holding Levi so Jamie Lynn could see how much he'd grown. "It means the world to me that you came to back me up. I promise I will take the best care of Levi."

Jamie Lynn smiled as Levi clasped her finger and gurgled.

"I will, as well," said Charli, coming up behind Henry and pressing a hand in between his shoulder blades. "And you can come visit him anytime."

"Thank you," said Jamie Lynn again. "But right now, as I mentioned in court, I'm headed for rehab. I hope to get clean for real this time. My life has completely spiraled out of control, and I realized after I had Levi that I was in no position to be a parent. You, though, Henry. I can't imagine a better parent for Levi than you. I'm so grateful."

"We'll be praying for you," he promised.

"And I'll pray for your little family," Jamie Lynn said in return.

And he was grateful for that. Becoming an instant husband and father, he needed all the help he could get.

Chapter Seventeen

Charli and Henry had gathered in the family room of the ranch house, summoned there by Martha. They sat side by side on the couch, Henry's arm tight around her shoulders and Levi on his lap. With all the hullabaloo around court, Charli hadn't spoken to her mother about the fire, and expected this meeting probably had something to do with it. She thought she was about to get reamed for her foolishness, maybe even have her proposal turned down flat.

Her mom came in and sat straight backed in the armchair facing them, her expression sober and her mouth in a thin, straight line.

"Are Fiona and Cordelia going to join us?" Charli asked.

Martha shook her head. "Not this time."

Suddenly, the air seemed to disappear from the room, and Charli gasped for breath. Though she'd known this moment would come, it still pierced her heart like a knife. "You wanted to talk to me about something?" She may as well just get it over with.

"You and Henry, yes," her mom said. "I've had the opportunity to speak with your sisters about your proposition where the ranch is concerned, and we've come to a decision regarding what we want to do going forward."

Henry pulled Charli closer under his arm. She thought he was having trouble taking a breath as well.

"I take full responsibility for the fire." Charli decided to lay it straight on the line. If they were about to yank everything out from under her, she needed them to know she understood. She had proven she didn't always make the best decisions where the ranch was concerned.

"What do you mean?" her mom demanded.

"Charli thinks it's all her fault the hay caught fire," Henry said. "I've tried to tell her otherwise, but she won't listen to me."

"Well, then, Charli. I hope you'll listen to your mother. I grew up on a ranch, and I know how many times random things happen that are beyond our control. All we can do is praise God when He cares for us in providential ways, as He did with that fire."

Charli's eyes remained dry, but her heart swelled with gratitude. "Thank you, Mom."

"Of course." She sounded like she was back to business, in her mom's typical way. "Now, let's talk about the ranch."

Charli couldn't find words, so she just nodded.

"After much discussion, and especially after that lovely trail ride, we realized just how much this ranch means to you. It's not about a career. It's about who you are as a person. We couldn't take that away from you. And who knows? Maybe I or your sisters will decide to make Hope our home."

"Really?" Charli's voice cracked.

"Yes. So we want you to keep the ranch. What you decide to do with it, including marrying Henry, is up to you. Your father's legacy belongs to you. Congratulations, Charli."

In her mind, she felt as if her father was suddenly there with her, holding out his hands and offering her the land.

Charli broke into tears.

Henry's heart was breaking for Charli, but for once it was in a good way. Sensing that this was a special moment, Martha had taken Levi and excused herself. As soon as she'd stepped from the room, Henry stood and pulled Charli to her feet, wrapping her in his arms and holding her tight.

"I feel as if Daddy is watching over me right now. He would be so happy."

"Of course he is," Henry said gently.

"I can't believe it."

"You did it, honey."

And then it hit him like a bullet, almost knocking him off his feet. She had done it. Not them. Her. She didn't need him anymore. She could do this without him.

Of course, he'd never leave her. He'd always be here to support her.

But she no longer needed to marry him to get the ranch.

He stepped back and brushed the pads of his thumbs across her wet cheeks.

"I'm crying," she said, but the words were full of joy.

"You are," he agreed with a soft smile. "It feels good to let it go, doesn't it?"

She nodded and sniffled.

"And now you can let all your worries go. You've got the ranch. Your dreams have come true. You don't need to do anything else."

Her gaze turned dark. "Henry? What are you talking about?" She sounded suspicious, as well she should be. The quicker he could clear this up, the better. Then he could leave and go do his own grieving.

"Your family has given you the ranch. And I have guardianship of Levi. I know we'll always be there for each other, but you no longer have to marry me."

She narrowed her gaze on him. "What are you going on about?"

"Exactly what I just said. You're free."

"I'm free," she repeated, not sounding as if she believed it. "Are you serious right now?"

"Absolutely." Even if inside his heart was smashing into a million shards of glass.

"Tell me how you really feel."

"Are you being sarcastic?" That wasn't like her.

"I'm absolutely being sarcastic, you goofball."

Charli never name-called, so this came as a huge surprise. It wasn't like her to be mean, if that's what she was doing.

Before he even knew what was happening, she'd wrapped her arms around his neck and her lips were on his. He couldn't help but react, melting into her.

What was happening right now?

When she broke away, she was beaming up at him. "Don't you know I'm in love with you? I finally figured out what Daddy meant in his letter to me, that love would find a way. It's my love for you and Levi. I'm glad we won the ranch, but I want to marry you with or without the land. You and Levi are my biggest blessings."

Henry couldn't believe what he was hearing. Despite his worst fears his dreams were coming true.

"I'm so blessed," he said, his voice thick with emotion. "And I love you so much. There's nothing I want more than for you to be my wife and Levi's mama. I know you've already asked me and we've made most of our plans, but I can't help but want to ask you again and seal the deal between us."

He framed her face with his hands and pressed his lips to hers before whispering, "Charli, my love, will you make me the happiest man in the world and marry me?"

* * * * *

*If you liked this story from Deb Kastner,
check out her previous Love Inspired books:*

Bonding with the Babies
A Reason to Stay
Their Unbreakable Bond

Available now from Love Inspired!

Find more great reads at www.LoveInspired.com.

Dear Reader,

Welcome to my new miniseries, Big Sky Legacy, set in the fictional mountain town of Hope, Montana. Last year I took a road trip up to Canada from my home in Colorado and completely fell in love with the scenery I passed. God really outdid Himself! I immediately realized I had to set my next series in Montana.

In *The Surprise Cowboy Dad*, heroine Charli is trying to come to terms with how she experienced grief over the passing of her beloved father. When I started the book, I had no idea just how real this would become for me. My own father passed away during this time, and like Charli, I've struggled to discover if there's a "right" way to mourn. For me, grief comes in waves. I'll think about my dad at the most unusual of times, and sometimes I can't hold back tears when my heart is breaking.

My father was the first one to introduce me to the love of books. Some of my first memories are of him snuggling me on a big, comfy armchair, singing and reading to me while we cuddled. He had a subscription to Reader's Digest Condensed Books, and I scarfed them down like a starving child, not knowing how it was introducing me to a variety of genres and giving me a great base upon which to build my love of reading.

I hope you enjoy Charli and Henry's story as much as I enjoyed writing it. Please visit my website at debkastnerbooks.com to sign up for my newsletter and connect to all my social media accounts. I would love to get to know you better, and I pray for you every day.

Dare to Dream,
Deb Kastner

Get up to 4 Free Books!

We'll send you 2 free books from each series you try PLUS a free Mystery Gift.

FREE Value Over **$25**

Both the **Love Inspired®** and **Love Inspired® Suspense** series feature compelling novels filled with inspirational romance, faith, forgiveness and hope.

YES! Please send me 2 FREE novels from the Love Inspired or Love Inspired Suspense series and my FREE gift (gift is worth about $10 retail). After receiving them, if I don't wish to receive any more books, I can return the shipping statement marked "cancel." If I don't cancel, I will receive 6 brand-new Love Inspired Larger-Print books or Love Inspired Suspense Larger-Print books every month and be billed just $7.19 each in the U.S. or $7.99 each in Canada. That is a savings of 20% off the cover price. It's quite a bargain! Shipping and handling is just 50¢ per book in the U.S. and $1.25 per book in Canada.* I understand that accepting the 2 free books and gift places me under no obligation to buy anything. I can always return a shipment and cancel at any time by calling the number below. The free books and gift are mine to keep no matter what I decide.

Choose one:
- ☐ **Love Inspired Larger-Print** (122/322 BPA G36Y)
- ☐ **Love Inspired Suspense Larger-Print** (107/307 BPA G36Y)
- ☐ **Or Try Both!** (122/322 & 107/307 BPA G36Z)

Name (please print)

Address   Apt. #

City   State/Province   Zip/Postal Code

Email: Please check this box ☐ if you would like to receive newsletters and promotional emails from Harlequin Enterprises ULC and its affiliates. You can unsubscribe anytime.

> Mail to the **Harlequin Reader Service:**
> **IN U.S.A.:** P.O. Box 1341, Buffalo, NY 14240-8531
> **IN CANADA:** P.O. Box 603, Fort Erie, Ontario L2A 5X3

Want to explore our other series or interested in ebooks? Visit www.ReaderService.com or call 1-800-873-8635.

*Terms and prices subject to change without notice. Prices do not include sales taxes, which will be charged (if applicable) based on your state or country of residence. Canadian residents will be charged applicable taxes. Offer not valid in Quebec. This offer is limited to one order per household. Books received may not be as shown. Not valid for current subscribers to the Love Inspired or Love Inspired Suspense series. All orders subject to approval. Credit or debit balances in a customer's account(s) may be offset by any other outstanding balance owed by or to the customer. Please allow 4 to 6 weeks for delivery. Offer available while quantities last.

Your Privacy—Your information is being collected by Harlequin Enterprises ULC, operating as Harlequin Reader Service. For a complete summary of the information we collect, how we use this information and to whom it is disclosed, please visit our privacy notice located at https://corporate.harlequin.com/privacy-notice. Notice to California Residents – Under California law, you have specific rights to control and access your data. For more information on these rights and how to exercise them, visit https://corporate.harlequin.com/california-privacy. For additional information for residents of other U.S. states that provide their residents with certain rights with respect to personal data, visit https://corporate.harlequin.com/other-state-residents-privacy-rights/.